A SEASON FOR FIREFLIES

ALSO BY REBECCA MAIZEL

Between Us and the Moon

REBECCA MAIZEL

HarperTeen is an imprint of HarperCollins Publishers.

A Season for Fireflies

 For information address HarperCollins Children's Books, a division of HarperCollins Publishers, 195 Broadway, New York, NY 10007.
www.epicreads.com

Library of Congress Control Number: 2016931027
ISBN 978-0-06-232764-2

Typography by Sarah Creech
16 17 18 19 20 PC/RRDH 10 9 8 7 6 5 4 3 2 1
❖
First Edition

For Mom

For the days you sat by the fire reading Jane Austen
and showing me what it means to love a story.
You never let me forget that I am special. I love you.

PART ONE

Sophomore Year
Late May

ONE

"CUT! CUT! CUT!" MS. TAFT SAYS WITH A SIGH. "I swear, you two are going to send me to an early grave."

She means Wes and me.

"Shouldn't have cast best friends for the leads," I hear from the front row, but before I can make a face at my other best friend, May, she sticks out her tongue at me. She's Hero in this spring's play, *Much Ado About Nothing*, and the velvet fabric of her dress spills over the armrest of the auditorium chair.

I've been standing on this stage since school ended two hours ago and I'm starving. I know it's nearly time for a dinner break but if I take my cell phone out of my pocket, Taft will confiscate it. Nearly on cue, it vibrates.

"Wes, don't reach for Penny's arm during this scene," Ms. Taft says, and walks onto the stage from the first row of auditorium seats. "I know I sound like a broken record, but Benedick doesn't know he's in love with Beatrice yet."

Wes takes a purposeful step back from me and sticks his hands in his pockets. Great. Nice work, Taft. He *always* sticks his hands in his pockets when someone is making him uncomfortable. The vibration against my hip bone buzzes again. *Get the hint, I am at rehearsal.* I silence it by pushing the top button without Taft seeing me.

Ms. Taft goes on. "The characters are still bickering and arguing as they always do, so it doesn't make sense for you to touch her like that, in such an affectionate way."

"Okay, okay, I got it," Wes says quickly.

"Ms. Taft," I say, stepping forward and overenunciating my words. "Wes isn't doing a very good job of *acting*."

"Oh, here we go," Taft says with a roll of her eyes. She's always telling me I like to share my opinion a little *too* much. But I just grin and turn to Wes.

"We're *actors*!" I say it really slowly and loud. "See, acting is when you pretend you're someone else and you—"

Wes steps forward and smacks me on the arm with his script. I jump away, laughing, when my phone buzzes yet again.

"Food's here!" May calls, and everyone drops what they are doing at the same time. Taft puts down her script. "I'm starving." She heads backstage, her curls flying behind her. I slip my phone out of my pocket.

"Penny!" Wes calls. "I have to talk to you." I shake the phone at him, signaling for him to wait a sec, and disappear behind the curtain. When I pick up, it's Bettie, my parents' housekeeper.

"Penny, I'm sorry to bother you," she says quickly after I say hello. "Have you heard from your dad? He's tried to call you. He's on his way home." I check the time. It's only 6:45 and Dad was supposed to be at the Best Of Rhode Island Gala with Mom. Her business was voted Best Event Planning and PR company in Rhode Island two weeks ago.

I step closer to the curtain so the fabric muffles my voice. I immediately think of wine bottles on the counter and the steep staircase in our house. The drinking wasn't so bad before. I barely remember her drinking when I was a kid. But the last two years, she drinks every night. "Is everyone okay?" I whisper.

"Your mom's okay, but she got into a very public screaming match with one of her client's mothers at the Gala. She *pushed* the woman. The news is planning to run a story. It's bad, honey. She's been ousted from her own company."

Ousted. Pushed.

"I'm here now and your dad is on his way—but I wanted you to know, honey. So you wouldn't be surprised when you got home."

She says something about "what I should expect when I get back" but she hangs up before I can hear anything in the background like voices or Mom crying.

When I step back out, May joins me but this time in her regular clothes.

"Pizza's here! Are you guys deaf?" She means Wes and me, as we are the only people left out here. It doesn't appear that Wes heard me on the phone, which is *good*.

"I'll be right back," Wes calls from the other side of the backstage. May loops her arm through mine. I touch her arm with my fingertips when I would really like to squeeze and have her tell me that my family hasn't been outed—that my mom is okay.

And it only occurs to me that I didn't know, right until this very second, that Mom's drinking had become a secret.

"It's pineapple pizza!" May sing-songs. "Your fave."

I can't even imagine Mom being drunk in public, especially at the Best Of party.

"Hello? Earth to Penny?" May says.

"Sorry! Just thinking about my lines," I lie but with a lift to my voice. I bury how I feel about Mom under the muscles, near the bones.

"What's up?" May nods to Wes. I shrug. When it comes to Wes and his love for inventing things lately, it could be anything.

"PS?" May whispers. "What was that about Wes touching you for the *third* time?" She unlatches from me and sits down on the stage. "He couldn't keep his hands off you."

"We were just doing the scene," I say.

I've been standing forever, and it's a relief to sit down.

"He's *always* touching you," May says.

"Uh, he's my best friend. Since eighth grade. Will you guys give it up already?"

People have been trying to get Wes and me together since we first met. May, Karen, Panda, and Richard—the whole theater crew. Wes has always waved it off so I haven't let myself believe it could be true. I've just pushed it to the side and kept myself in check. We're good at laughing, at acting, and at being best friends. I haven't wanted to screw it up between us.

If he didn't want me, I wouldn't be able to hide his rejection the way I hide Mom's drinking.

Bettie's voice rings through my head again. *Ousted. Public screaming match.*

Wes comes back out carrying a cardboard box in his hands. He's changed back into his street clothes, so he's wearing a T-shirt and jeans. His forearms flex as he puts the box down, and when he looks up at me, he smiles with his tongue sticking out of the side of his mouth. His eyes glint in their devilish way.

Damn it. I've let May brainwash me.

"Can you handle that, Gumby?" I say, shaking off Bettie's words ringing in my head and the yelling voices that will no doubt be filling the house when I get there. Wes's arms wrap around the box. He's not all arms and legs like he was in eighth grade when he got that nickname. It doesn't really fit anymore.

"Got it, doll," he says, and makes sure to emphasize the word.

A flick of fire rushes through me.

"I am *no one's* doll," I snap.

"Ooh, did I hit a nerve, toots?"

"Toots?" I should kick him.

"Honey? Babyface?" he calls from where I can't see him.

"I'll show you a baby face!" I cry back.

"Don't get her started!" May says with a cackle. "Though she be but little, she is fierce!"

"Stay right there, dollface," Wes calls. His footsteps make loud thumps backstage because he's gotten so damn big lately.

With a sharp *click* the stage and front row of the auditorium fall into darkness. The track lighting in the aisles gives the room a frosty gray halo, but the light doesn't quite reach the whole stage.

I can see the outline of the cardboard box from where I sit. Wes bends over and pulls out some kind of contraption—a small globe on a black base. Even though Wes is large, he's gentle as he places the globe quietly onto the stage.

"Okay, okay, this is it," he says, and even though his features are cast in shadow, I can tell that he's smiling.

"Can we hurry it up? I'd like to eat pizza sometime today," May groans.

It's amazing that I was so hungry five minutes ago. Bettie called and I've completely lost my appetite.

"So, remember the other night. At the beach?" Wes says, and a whoosh of adrenaline sweeps through me at the memory. Of course I remember. I lied. I told them I just wanted to go to the beach when really Mom was drinking again and I just didn't want to be home.

That night, Wes, Panda, May, and Karen came to get me in Wes's minivan. We drove out to Narragansett Beach and lay out looking at the stars. We were just us. The four of us laughing and making fun of Taft, like always. I didn't bring Mom up and no one asked. It was perfect. Until now.

"On the beach," Wes continues, "you said you wished the stars weren't so far away, that it wasn't fair." Even in the dark, his voice sounds happy. "So I built this," he finishes.

"Because of what I said?" I say, and my voice wavers.

With a little *click* on the globe, a swirl of purple, green, and silver stars projects against the black curtains.

Clusters of silver stars rotate in a slow trance. Galaxies shift in and out of view—blue, then pink, then silver circling again and again. The universe really could be right here on our stage. And maybe in some ways, it is.

Wes *made* me a planetarium?

"This beats the glow-in-the-dark stars on my ceiling," May says from the space on my left. Wes lies down on the other side of me, laughing. I'm surprised how strong his laughter is and . . . how deep.

"Unbelievable," I whisper at the stars, careful not to look over at Wes. I'm not sure if I'm talking about the buzzing energy between us or the stars on the ceiling. Something about looking at Wes while lying down in the dark is too much for me right now. It's almost enough to make me forget about Mom and what awaits me when I get home.

"Is Penny actually speechless?" May says. I keep my eyes on the constellations.

"I got the images of the constellations to project at the highest possible resolution," Wes explains proudly as the stars and planets circle overhead.

"Some of the stars look like little fireflies," May says quietly.

"Guys!" Taft pokes her head around the curtain. "Come eat, we only have time for a ten-minute break. Oh *cool*!" she says, and her eyes lift to the constellations. "You know"—she motions to the stars with her pizza crust—"we could use that if we did *Midsummer Night's Dream*."

Taft disappears and I hear snippets of chatter from backstage. My stomach growls properly. Maybe I could eat a slice. I offer May my hand and we stand up.

"What do you think, Berne?" Wes says once he's up and packing the planetarium away in a box.

Again, my eyes flick to his muscles as he picks up the box and places it on a counter backstage. He really *has* been working out. How have I never noticed it before? I wonder what it would be like to kiss him.

"What do I think?" I fall into step with him, and we make our way to the dressing room, following the laughter and the smell of pizza. I want to say how much I love the planetarium, how important it is that he *heard* me that night. I struggle to say thank you, but looking him in the eye to say something so true stops my words.

"You've got too much time on your hands," I say instead, and punch him lightly in the shoulder. He looks a little hurt. "I'm kidding. Thank you."

"Always, Berne," he says. The spark that I love is back behind his eyes. May pulls on my hand, drawing me back a bit to let Wes walk ahead. Once he's out of earshot, she nudges me with her elbow.

"You better be excited," she says.

"For what? He's getting really good at . . ." I search for a word that makes sense. "Crafts. That's all it is."

May raises an eyebrow.

"He's just into building contraptions right now," I insist. "He wanted to build that tree thing for *Much Ado*."

I wink at her and skip through the doorway of the dressing room before I can hear what she says in response.

"Bonjour!" I cry out, and leap to the table of pizza like a ballerina. *"Comment allez-vous?"* I curtsy at the small smattering of applause and pull a pizza slice onto a paper plate. I sit down in a seat next to Karen and make sure to pull a chair close for May. My cell phone vibrates in my pocket again, but I ignore it. I just have to get through rehearsal. Then I can think about what's happening at home.

"Do you ever enter a room normally?" Karen laughs, and takes a bite of her pizza.

"No," May answers for me, sitting down on my other side.

We listen to Panda describe a video game that none of us have ever heard of. Panda's boyfriend, Richard, shakes his head in mock disapproval. He has such a calming presence next to Panda's loud joking and laughter. Richard's skin is a rich brown, made even deeper by the royal blue of his shirt. Wes sits down beside Richard and leans forward to hear the conversation. As I take my first bite of pineapple pizza, May tilts her head closer so her hair lightly touches my cheek. "Blow me off *all* you want, Berne. Do your normal 'it's no big deal' thing like you always do. But"—she lowers her voice and nods to Wes on the other side of the room—"thou knowest he did it for you."

TWO

MY MOTHER IS ON THE SCREEN. SHE'S IN THE glittering dress she wore to the Best Of party. She steps from the curb with her assistant, Lacey, and she stumbles onto the street, nearly headfirst. Lacey tries to pick her up from under her arm but she shoves Lacey and falls into the car.

I flinch, wanting to reach out and catch her.

The news runs the story about Mom for two or three days. During class on Monday, May asked if I wanted to talk about it, but I quickly changed the subject to rehearsal. Panda brought it up at rehearsal, but I spotted Richard across the parking lot and called him over, abruptly ending our conversation.

I've been trying to focus on other things.

"I'm telling you. He's been avoiding me since Tuesday," I say. I'm on the phone with May on Saturday, days later. It's finally the start of tech week. I snatch up pants, T-shirts, and some toothpaste so I can brush my teeth before scenes. I shove them into a duffel bag to bring to school. Rehearsal started ten minutes ago.

"You're opposite one another in the play. How can he avoid you?" May asks.

"You know what I mean," I say. "Ever since the planetarium light show, he's been all weird. He's conveniently missing during breaks and I haven't seen him at lunch."

"Well, get your ass here. Taft is freaking out about you being late," May says, and I can tell she's brushing her teeth backstage—her pre-rehearsal ritual—because her words are garbled.

"My dad is still at work. I need to get my mom to drive me," I say. "I'm almost out the door."

May inhales like she is going to ask me something, but she doesn't.

"Two weeks until I am free from permit land." I say quickly and lift the heavy duffel with a groan. "Gotta go. See you soon." I hang up before May can ask if Mom is okay to drive. I don't even know if she's okay. She hasn't left the house in a week. I walk into the kitchen.

"Mom!" I call.

Out of habit, I check Mom's work calendar that hangs in the kitchen above the messy counter. Bettie always cleans up the empty wine bottles Mom leaves lying around, but today she left at four, so there are two. There's a bottle of white in the sink that's empty, and one on the counter that's half-finished. Mom's not going anywhere tonight.

Maybe I can drive myself. I only have my permit, but our town is small and if I drive carefully, I should be fine. I can't ask Wes to come pick me up. He can't see Mom like this. Sure, he's seen her glassy-eyed, but Mom's always been dressed up in her pearls and hiding her sadness behind designer clothes. It's when the doors are closed, the events are over, and the house is empty that a dark room is her favorite place to be. Since she's been fired, that's the new normal.

When I'm at the kitchen table, zipping up my bag, my cell goes off a few more times: May, Panda, and Taft, asking where I am. The last is a text from Wes.

WES: Should I get u?

I look around at the empty kitchen, the quiet house. Mom must be up in her room. Maybe if Wes comes to get me there's a chance he won't see her. My fingers hover over the phone, but then Mom comes into the room, holding her cell phone and a wineglass. That's the same blouse and pants she was wearing yesterday. Third time this week that she hasn't changed clothes.

"Mom?" I say. "Are you okay?"

She hip checks the island and places the phone and glass down, messily, so the base of the wineglass rocks back and forth. I reach out to keep it from falling to the floor. I could tell Wes he can't come in, that I'll meet him outside. That would be awkward too and he would want to know why.

Mom moves to grab the second bottle. It glugs as she pours a big glass.

"Are you sure you want more?" I ask. I try to choose my words really carefully. No judgment.

"I'll decide when I've—" she starts, and rests her hand on the island but slips on a puddle of wine on the counter. I run to help her, but she catches herself on her elbow with a smack. Her eyes are heavy, but open. I should call Bettie. I can't leave her like this and go to rehearsal. She can't be alone.

Mom tries to stand. She reaches for the wine bottle and glass, but I move them out of her way. "Mom, stop it. You can barely walk."

"I'm fine!" She snatches the bottle.

"No, you're not!" I cry, and grab for it. Her fingers let go easily. She doesn't fight me on it, just takes the glass she just poured, which I didn't think to grab in time.

She makes her way out of the kitchen with the glass in her hand, and what sucks is that I have to let her. If I don't, she could get all the way upstairs, realize she wants some wine, and try to come back downstairs—and she is *not* in good enough shape for that. I fight the urge to help her, because she seems so intent on doing it herself. She's moving too fast, her shoulder hits the doorframe, her head ricochets, and it all seems to happen before I can react. There's a hard *thud* and she falls, smacking the back of her head on the floor. The glass clatters and rolls away, the wine spilling everywhere. At least the glass doesn't shatter.

"Aw," she moans. "Ow . . ."

I pick up my cell to call Bettie, but see May's name on the screen calling me instead.

"Penny. Where *are* you?" May hisses. "What's going on? Is it your mom? Penny, is it?"

Mom drools on herself a little, so some white syrup spit-up dribbles onto her blouse. I pull her up from the floor by her elbow. "I'll be there soon, May. I'm sorry. Tell Taft."

I hang up and dial Bettie's number. I wish Dad were here. Mom isn't as bad when Dad is home.

"Come on, Mom," I say, and try to help her stand as the phone rings on the other end. She does stand a little, relieving her body weight from my arms. "You can do it."

Mom's legs slip, but with my help she pulls herself up and stumbles to the stairs. She struggles against me. "Stop!" she yells. "Give me my wine." Her eyes focus, her eyebrows are angular and V-shaped.

Bettie's voice barely touches the air when I cut her off. "Bettie. It's my mom. She's—"

"I'm coming. I'm coming," she says, and hangs up.

"My drink. Where is it?" Mom says, though it's slurred.

"Sorry, but there isn't any left," I lie, and we make our way up the stairs. Mom leans on me, but I push her forward so she doesn't fall back.

"*You* broke the bottle . . ." Mom starts, but doesn't finish. When we get to her bedroom she collapses onto the bed and crawls on all fours toward her pillows.

"You're so *difficult*," Mom says as she slumps against them. She's frowning, her eyes are unfocused. She always says I'm difficult. "You're too much" is her favorite expression.

"The stress of your endless *demands*." Some spit flies out of her mouth into an arc in the air.

"What are you talking about?" I say.

"Always so *demanding*."

There's that word again.

"*Relentless*. You just *need* me all the time."

"I have rehearsal," I say, trying to stop her tirade. I back away toward the stair landing.

"Fired because of *you*. Drink because of *you*." A little spittle flies out again. "If you weren't so difficult, I wouldn't have to relax. I just need five minutes to myself," she mumbles. I want to defend myself—want to tell her she's wrong. But then I think about how each time we fight about something stupid—clothes I need for school, rehearsal schedules—she gets a headache and has to go lie down. She always grabs a bottle of wine on her way. Is it me? Did I really drive her to this?

Somewhere inside my head, a voice whispers . . . *yes*.

"Penny?" Bettie's voice rings out from the kitchen.

Mom's eyes are already closed and she's curled her knees to her chest. She's mumbling but I can't hear it, thank god.

I pass Bettie on the stairs. She stops me with a strong hand on my shoulder.

I don't want to look at her watery blue eyes or her unkempt, off-hours hair. I really don't want her to see me right now. "Is she okay?" she asks.

I search the fibers in the carpet beneath my feet to try to answer that question.

"I have rehearsal," is all I get out. Bettie reaches out to me, but I pull away. "Is it okay that I go?" She answers me with an "Of course," and I will thank her for this help, not at all in her job description, in my usual way. A small note and doing extra chores.

I walk to my car and place my theater bag in the passenger seat.

If you weren't so difficult.

I illegally drive the 2.1 miles to school.

Because of you.

It's warm out and twilight threatens the sunny Saturday afternoon as I walk into the theater.

"Penny!" May calls from the stage.

"We're saved!" Panda cries, and everyone laughs. I search for Wes briefly but I don't see him. Everyone is in costume.

Taft flies down the aisle at me, curls bouncing.

"Hallway," she says, and points at the door I came through.

When we're on the other side of the door, Taft crosses her arms. "What is going on?"

There are crisscrosses in the pattern of the linoleum beneath my feet.

"What happened? This isn't like you, I'm worried," she presses. "We've all seen the news. Is everything okay at home?"

I look up into her eyes, but don't have the words to say what's happened. I am glad Bettie's helping to pick up the pieces now. But it won't end there. It will still be tech week, then performance, and Mom will still think I am demanding. She'll come to the performance drunk. Panic rushes through me and I take a rattled breath but don't want to explain.

"Well, I can't make you talk. But you need to keep me posted, Penny. Especially if you are going to—" Ms. Taft pauses and seems to choose her words carefully. "If you can't make it here on time."

I just need five minutes to myself.

"Forget the costume for right now, let's run it through the Beatrice and Benedick scene from yesterday."

A few moments later I stand onstage. May, as Hero, has just exited the stage and stands down at the first row of seats. Mr. Hill, our physics teacher and resident tailor, fixes something at the elbow of her costume. She's frowning at me because I haven't told her what's wrong, even though she basically already knows, just like everyone else.

"Okay, places," Taft instructs.

I close my eyes, try to steel myself for the love I'm meant to feel in this scene. As Beatrice, I have to let the audience know that, even while I come off as cold and disdainful, it's all just an act so no one will know the truth, that deep down I love Benedick.

"Ready with the spotlight, Panda?" Taft calls.

"I've got a faulty switch up here," he calls back. "We need to get to the fuse box."

Taft sighs. "It's always something," she says, and her heels clip on the stage as she makes her way up to the light booth.

I stay on my spike mark because I know Taft needs me to be in position for the spotlight. I cross my arms over my chest. In a few minutes, I'm supposed to dance and skip around the stage—in love.

Wes stands in the wings. He's got on a flowy white shirt as part of his costume but Taft has let him wear his jeans instead of the tights and breeches.

Our eyes meet.

I imagine myself on the stage, in front of everyone as Beatrice, skipping and crying out, "Benedick, love on; I will requite thee, taming my wild heart to thy loving hand!"

We share a smile, one that I put on for his benefit. When I look away to the empty auditorium, I whisper a different one of Beatrice's lines instead:

"For truly, I love none."

The Elizabethan English feels forced. I don't want to be on a stage right now. I don't want anyone to look at me. To guess how I am feeling or what might be happening at home.

"Penny."

Wes is next to me.

"You okay?" His voice is full of concern. I don't say anything when he steps closer to me. Instead, I focus on his lips. They're beautiful, actually. I suppose if I let myself, and we were alone, I could lean over, kiss him, and then I wouldn't have to think of something to say. He would know how I feel.

He wipes his mouth. "Is there something on my face?"

I shake my head and pull back.

"Penny, say something. It's not like you to be quiet," he says. I'm grateful for the loud chatter from the cast in the background, filling the silence.

I clear my throat. "I'm just tired."

May comes up the stairs to the stage too and has to lift the heavy material and hem of the skirt. "What's going on?"

"Nothing."

May rolls her eyes.

My cheeks warm. I don't want to have to tell them how bad it's gotten and the terrible truth Mom confessed tonight. My friends have always joked with me, called me "drama queen" or "intense." I thought we were just kidding around, but maybe—maybe they were right. Maybe Mom is right.

"What happened tonight? And don't tell me that everything is fine when we both know it isn't," May says. "I've seen the news. We all have."

Even though it's air-conditioned in here, I'm burning up.

"Is it the play?" May says.

"Is it your lines?" Wes counters.

She's not talking.

Why isn't she talking?

I don't know.

You look like you've been crying. Have you been crying?

They ask me question after question but none of them are the right one. I'm afraid if I open my mouth to answer even one of them, I'll break down. And that would be the worst possible thing. I'm an actress so I *don't* have to show people the real me.

"I don't want to talk about it!" I snap. They both flinch. Wes digs his hands in his pockets with a nod to the floor. I glance out at the audience—everyone is looking at me. The chatter has stopped.

"What *do* you want to talk about?" he says. His eyes are on me. I want to ask him why he's been avoiding me. I want to ask him what he meant with the star projector.

When I glance behind me at the wings of the stage, Richard, dressed as Claudio, is watching us. He turns away and pretends to be inspecting a thread on his costume.

What am I going to do? I don't know if I can call Bettie every *single* time. What if Bettie up and quits? Dad's at work most of the time and when he's home, he pretends everything is normal. I can't do this alone.

"Tell me," May insists. "You have that look in your eye. Like you had a fight with your mom."

She can tell just by looking at me? What if everyone can tell? What if I get up on stage and the whole audience knows? I have a *look in my eye* that gives away when I've had a fight with Mom. I'm off the stage. I rush down the stairs to the carpeted aisle and up to the hallway.

"Penny!" Taft and May call nearly in unison.

"Where is she going?" Taft cries from up in the lighting booth.

I run down the hallway toward the exit. Once I get out of the double doors to the parking lot, I hear them slam open again and Wes's heavy footsteps following behind me.

I stop next to my car. I can't be on a stage, out there, exposed in front of everyone. The thought of telling them about Mom makes a burning hole in the center of my belly. I just want to hide, where my secret is safe, tucked under the muscles. Hurting only me.

I shake my head at the reflection in my car window. Wes walks up behind me.

"You are acting like a psycho," Wes says. I turn to face him.

"Why did you ignore me this week?" I don't mean to blurt this, but it just rushes out.

He shoves his hands in his pockets and I know what this means.

I can feel the heat in my cheeks and there's a point in the center of my chest that's pinging. Tears make my nose tingle and I try to stop them by taking deep breaths.

"Berne, you're killing me," he says, but I hate the tone in his voice that I can't identify.

"Why?"

"I didn't ignore you."

"Then what's going on?"

"I've been trying to figure out a way . . ." Wes's voice trails off. I look up, waiting for him to say something, anything. Maybe I can tell him what's going on. He could dig deep, into my bones where my secrets are hiding, if he wanted. I might be able to pry myself open for Wes.

"I haven't wanted to be *just* friends for a long time, you know that," he says quietly, and his blue eyes lift to mine.

But then I think, if we got together, he would come over much more often. Wes would see firsthand how bad it is. He'd feel sorry for me or worse—he'd agree with her. No way. It's too much.

"Say something," he says.

"I gotta go," I say quickly.

"Go?"

"I can't," I say.

"Be with me?" he says.

"No, I mean—be in the play."

I don't continue because May shoves her way out the doors

of school, in full costume, and rushes to us, her long black hair flying behind her.

I turn to open the door to my car, fumbling my keys. They drop with a hard *clang* to the ground. When I pick them up, May is next to us.

"Penny is apparently quitting the play," Wes says with a shake of his head. His cheeks are flushed. "A week before opening night."

"I just need to think this through," I say.

"Are you on drugs?" May cries. "*You're* quitting the play. You *are* the play!"

"It's too much," I say.

"Penny Berne. You've done theater since you were six years old. And now you're quitting. For *no* reason." With sharp movements, she pulls her hair back in a long black ponytail. I've never seen May so furious. Her small features seem to transform when she's angry—they become hard angles. May always gets angry right away when something happens she can't control. But this is different. This is my problem. *I'm* the cause of the problem.

May crosses her arms over her chest. "Maybe you should actually tell someone what's wrong," May says. "You're being really selfish, Penny. Keeping your secrets and acting like everything is fine. And then you come here like a complete freak—"

"May, stop," Wes scolds.

"She's right," I croak.

"You're damn right, I'm right! So keep your stupid secrets. Have fun telling Taft you're quitting a week before opening night. That should go over real well. Excuse me, I have to go learn Beatrice's damn lines, so I can be your understudy." May stalks away and my bottom lip trembles like I'm five so I turn away and get into my car. I don't look at Wes, *can't* look at Wes, so I get in my car and head home.

Dad's car is in the driveway right next to Mom's. It's dark in the kitchen; all the wine and remnants of Mom's spill have been cleaned up. I don't know when Bettie left, but it's clear she made it look nice in here.

"Penny." Dad calls my name from the living room. I step across the kitchen to where he sits on the couch with a mug of coffee. He gestures to the love seat across from him. "Bettie told me what happened tonight."

I wonder how much Bettie heard when Mom was yelling at me, but Dad continues, "I need you to sit down, kiddo."

I do. I'm exhausted.

"What's going on?" I ask.

"I can't take it anymore, Pen. And neither can you. So," he says, and takes a deep breath, "when your mom gets up, I'm going to take her to the hospital."

"Is she okay? Did she fall?"

"Not that kind of hospital. Your mom needs to get herself better. The combination of the pills she takes and the alcohol she drinks make it dangerous for her to be left alone. Especially with you."

"You always said there was nothing you can do."

"It's not good for you to be in this environment," Dad says, and it almost sounds rehearsed, like he's been practicing this conversation. "I can't always be here with work, and Bettie shouldn't have to be responsible for Mom."

I want to guess where he's going but I can't. "I'm going to insist that we bring Mom to a rehab facility." Dad rests his elbows on his knees. That's how he sits during business calls.

Rehab facility. The words settle in my head. I don't even know what it entails exactly, just that it's where people go when they need to get off drugs. I know things are bad, but I've never thought this might be real—that she could be an *alcoholic.*

"She doesn't even drink all the time," I say, and I hear myself making the same excuses Dad does whenever I bring up her drinking.

"I know, Pen, but it's enough."

I swallow hard. My throat is sore from my fight with Wes and May. "She'll never agree."

Dad exhales deeply and wipes his hand over his bald head. He cleans his glasses when he says, "She has to. If she wants to be a part of this family."

"You'll just kick her out?" My voice breaks.

"Do you want her falling down? Hurting you?" He doesn't even know that this is my fault. She wouldn't be drinking if I wasn't so dramatic all the time, if I wasn't so endlessly demanding.

"Maybe I can help out with chores more? I quit the play, so I'll be around more. I can help Mom with some stuff around the house. I can get Bettie to take me to get clothes or supplies or whatever. I won't be as stressful."

Dad shakes his head at his hands folded on his knees. His voice softens and he says in a low voice, "You think this has anything to do with you?" I nod. "It's really important she gets help, hon. She's sick."

"Arthur?" Mom's ragged, sleepy voice calls from upstairs. I don't want to be here to see this. I can't. Dad gets up to go to her. "Penny!" he calls, but I'm out the door.

I drive fast through the neighborhood just as the streetlamps pop on. They light the way like torches to my dock, the one I go to whenever I need a minute to get my head on straight. The summer air is thick and humid. I zip past the bait and tackle shops, the Greenwich Boat Company, and the broken and dismembered carcasses of motorboats in the yard. I finally turn onto Main Street faster than the speed limit, pull into a parking spot, and when I get out, I walk fast through town.

I walk a bit, breathing deeply. Someone has strewn twinkle lights across the top of the lampposts and they hang over the street. WELCOME SUMMER FESTIVAL posters are taped on each storefront window. Next to me is the Coffee Stop, which throws a hazy light onto the street. Inside, Kylie Castelli and her usual crew sit in the big red booth in the front. The table faces Main Street and they eat from a Make Your Own S'mores platter, laughing and dipping fruit and candy in the melted chocolate. Kylie wears a blue baseball hat backward and her blond hair falls in two long braids down her black tank top. She has gooey marshmallow on her fingers and waves them in the face of Eve Dennings, who I have never talked to and who I doubt would ever have a reason to talk to me. They seem happy.

My phone has been ringing off and on for the last hour.

I can't bring myself to answer.

I walk past the rowdy Fish Hook Tavern, to the marina where my dock waits. Some people relax on their boats; the bigger ones are on the A and B docks. Fireflies dot the sky and bob in the darkness of the trees in the woods across the water. My feet echo on the wooden planks down to the last dock, E. The one where Dad used to keep his boat before he got too busy and put it in storage.

When I get to the end, there are two posts about six feet high on either side that anchor the dock in place. The water laps against the underside and I sit down, running through the last few days in my head. After about half an hour, I hear footsteps coming down the dock.

Wes sits down next to me.

"I knew you'd come here eventually," he says.

I look out at the shifting water and some of the fireflies that maneuver out in the woods across the harbor.

"I know you don't want to talk, but I had to make sure you were okay," he says. He reaches for my hand and it's the first time he's ever reached for me like *this.* "I know what the news is saying about your mom's company. And I've seen your mom when she's being hard on you."

I get up, dropping his hand, and take a step back to the pole behind me.

"Don't look at me like that, Penny," he says, standing up too. "It's cool. She's always been nice to me."

His honesty makes me cringe. How many times has he seen things, like May had, that I haven't wanted him to? That I thought I could cover up?

He takes a step to me and I can't back away any farther or I'll be in the water.

He lifts his hand to my cheek and one of my tears rolls over his fingers.

"It's not a secret. You don't have to hide it. Especially not from me."

Now our chests are touching. My heart is pounding so hard, I'm surprised his shirt isn't vibrating from the force.

Wes slips his hand behind my head. He pulls me forward, just slightly, angling his head. I want to kiss him so badly that it makes my breath shudder. He hesitates before our lips touch. His eyes examine my face and I can barely see his blue eyes through the tears.

"I don't want the first time we kiss to be when you're crying, Penny," he whispers. "Just tell me what's going on."

"I'm sorry," I say. I know this is for the best.

In my head, I invent a scenario where Mom is in the passenger seat of Dad's car with a small designer bag filled with some sweaters and a small bottle of perfume. She is going to the rehab facility where she won't know anyone. The nurses won't know she likes a half of grapefruit for breakfast. She likes honey and sugar on her grapefruit too but it has to be *just right*. She tells me that I'm the only one who gets the ratio just how she likes it. A surge of love for Mom overwhelms me.

Wes lets out a frustrated sigh. "You know, if you don't start telling people what's wrong, it'll eat you up. One day you'll be exactly like your mom," he says. His words sting. I pull back and wipe a tear away.

"You don't know a damn thing about my mom," I say.

He's hurt. "I didn't mean—"

"Just go."

He says nothing further. Just walks up the dock to the street. I wish I could rewind this whole day, so I'm not angry with Wes too, but what he said is *exactly* why I can't say anything.

I can't tell him what he wants to hear, and he shouldn't have to pull the truth out of me. And the truth is that I don't want to be the person I've always been. I don't want to be the girl who leaps into a room and always gets the lead in every play, who comes alive when everyone is watching her. I don't feel like that girl anymore.

It's better here in a different kind of light—I look up to the moonlight shining down on the water and the dock. The stars twinkle above—far away and untouchable. My gut aches at the memory of Wes's planetarium. He wants to give me the stars, but I don't want people to try to fix me.

The truth is simple:

I want to be out of the spotlight.

For good.

THREE

A SURPRISING LATE-MORNING THUNDERSTORM IS pouring rain down so thick that most people have pulled over to the side of the road. I made it from the track to my car in just a minute but am soaked through so my shorts and now the car seat are totally drenched. Steam rises from the hot asphalt and as I pull out of the parking lot, I'm reminded of a time on the beach with Mom and Dad. The clouds came up as fast as I'd ever seen them and the sky opened up, pouring down on people's lunches and towels. Didn't seem to bother the seagulls though, who ate all the leftover sandwiches and chips.

My phone is silent as I make my way home. In the past week, no one has reached out to me much. Not May, not

Panda, and definitely not Wes.

Again, I'm driving with just my permit. At this point, following the rules is pretty low on my list of stuff to care about. Dad has been in the office more than ever since Mom entered the rehab facility. The person I see most consistently is Bettie, who makes breakfast for Dad and me every morning. We can't see Mom for a few days but I've talked to her a couple of times on the phone. I never mention what she confessed that other night—why she drinks.

I take the long way home down Diamond Hill Road so I don't have to drive past school. It's the second night of *Much Ado About Nothing.* I know Wes, Panda, May, and Karen won't see me at the bottom of the hill but I haven't talked to my friends since the night I ran out of the theater, and I don't want to take any chances of running into them.

Not since I quit the play.

I grip the steering wheel harder. Taft made me meet with her; the school counselor, Ms. Winters; and Headmaster Lewis. It didn't change my mind. I felt better actually when I heard people in the halls raving about May's performance as Beatrice.

I said nothing about the other night when Mom was drunk. I haven't had to; the news has done a stellar job of running "Alice Berne Updates" and even did an "on-site" broadcast last night from in front of the rehab facility. It's not like Mom is a national celebrity, but here in Rhode Island, the smallest state ever—Mom is a socialite. She always has great clothes, impressive celebrity clients, and knows how to put on an incredible event.

I keep on down Diamond Hill Road, taking the turns slowly.

The rush of water hurls down the slope of the steep street. The road is a curvy S shape and when I get down to the bottom, next to the edge of the woods, a gray Toyota Corolla is parked, idling with steam coming from the hood. Kylie Castelli kicks at the car and screams but I can't hear her over the rain. I pull up and stop behind her car.

I get out, noting a bumper sticker that reads, *Well Behaved Women Rarely Make History.* Kylie always knows the trends before they happen; she's constantly papering the hallway with band names I've never heard of and stickers of shows she's been to over the weekend. She has like two hundred movie and concert tickets taped inside her locker.

Kylie is on her knees and it looks like she has on brown knee guards from all the mud. Her tire is shredded—completely gone. She got out the jack, which I'm somewhat surprised by, and she's trying to lift the car up to change the tire.

"What happened?" I ask, and then decide that question is stupid.

She doesn't answer and with a shriek she pushes as hard as she can on the jack. She pushes too hard, throwing her off balance and onto her butt. Mud splashes onto her backside and legs.

"Well, balls," she says. I laugh and am surprised how strange it feels in my mouth. I haven't laughed, not for real anyway, since rehearsal. Her eyes lift up to mine and we're both smiling. Her usually perfectly tousled, messy-cool hair is matted on her forehead.

"Penny, right?" she says, and gets up.

We've been in Honors English together for two years, but I'm still surprised she knows my name. We've never spoken outside of class.

"Where's your spare?" I ask.

"The spare?"

"The spare tire," I clarify.

She shrugs. "Maybe the trunk?"

We stand at the back of the Toyota. I lift the trunk open and in between the gym clothes, EG Private track uniforms, and empty water bottles, there is no spare tire. I shut the trunk before everything in there gets soaked.

"You'll need to call a tow truck. Do you have the num—" I say, but I'm interrupted by an enormous crash of thunder.

"My cell died," she yells.

I motion to my car. When we get in, I hand my cell over. She says thanks as she takes it and I wish I could cover the dumb stickers on my glove box: *Globe Theatre*, *Shakespeare Rocks!*, *Keep Calm and Go to the Theatre*. Kylie drips water all over the seat.

"Mom? I got a flat," she says into the phone.

I can hear high-pitched squawking through the line.

"Yeah, give me a minute," Kylie says to the person on the phone, and motions to me for a pen. I reach across her to dig in the glove box, throwing playbills, old scripts, disposable toothbrushes to the floor and on top of her mud-covered pink-manicured toes. I hand the pen over, feeling like an oaf.

"Thanks," she says with a sigh, and hangs up. "My mother is a beast but she's calling Triple A for me."

I want to tell her I know all about beasts, but Kylie leans back in the seat, crossing one dirty leg over the other, and says,

"God, I *hate* my car. Is this a Lexus?"

"Um, yeah. My mom's old car."

"Jesus, you're lucky."

"I'm not technically supposed to be driving for another week."

"Are you a Cancer?" she says, and jumps in her seat a little.

"Yes?" I say after a moment of trying to keep up with her.

"Me too! June twenty-seventh."

"Twenty-fourth," I say. We're both driving when we shouldn't be, and smile.

"Aren't you going to get in trouble with Triple A for driving without a licensed driver?" I ask.

She ignores my question and continues to check out my car, flipping the visor up and down, and I keep thinking she'll get out eventually and go back to her car, but she doesn't. Instead, she plugs her cell phone into my car charger.

"Aren't you in the play or something?" she asks.

"I was. I . . ." I somehow think telling Kylie I quit anything is only going to make this more awkward.

"I used to be in theater," she says. "When I was little. My mom took me to some of the plays you were in at Ocean State." She means Ocean State Theater Company, where I first met May and Panda and was a kid actor in every free minute of my summers. I didn't meet Wes until eighth grade. "I wanted to *be* you," she adds.

What? I laugh, tipping my head back. "Are you kidding?"

I'm pretty sure everyone wants to be Kylie Castelli. Head of radio broadcasting at our school, dance committee treasurer, most likely to achieve greatness with a perfect tan.

"Anyway, I thought you'd be with your usual gaggle," she says.

"My gaggle? Don't *you* usually travel in a pack?"

She laughs. "Touché." She leans forward and touches the Globe Theatre sticker on my dash with a fingertip. Her nails are a mess of chipped polish. "I went to the Globe in London," she says. I must seem surprised. "What?" she says. "I like culture. I don't have to memorize lines like you do to love the theater. It's not my thing anymore, but it's still cool." She lifts her eyes to me with a tiny smile. "Okay, my mom made me go when we went on a trip there. But I liked it!" she says through laughter.

Kylie texts something on her phone quickly. I look to my hands because I don't have anyone to text. I'm not sorry I quit the play. I'm sorry that I've been blowing off May and Panda and Wes's calls.

"Shit, did I offend you? Words fly out of my mouth. I'm always doing damage control," Kylie says.

I shake my head. "No," I say. "It's just . . ."

She looks over at me, waiting. Kylie isn't afraid of anything. She rolls her hand, gesturing for me to go on.

"I quit the play," I admit.

"*You?* Miss I Do Monologues on Command in the Hallway?"

"Yeah . . . it hasn't been my best week."

"Is it because your mom got sent to rehab?"

I drop my head. "Yep. That's part of it. Guess you know from the news."

"Everyone knows. Fuck!" Kylie cries and the sound in the car echoes, even with the rain lightening up. "I am so tired of this town!" She brings her feet up against the dash and slaps her hands against her wet legs. "Aren't you?"

I nod. Her energy is infectious and I want to scream and curse and put my feet up on the dash, too.

"Whatever happened," she says gently, "I am sure you had your reasons."

She's not going to push. She's not hawk-eyeing me and I again nod, but this time, I meet her eyes.

"You need cheering up, Penny Berne," Kylie says, and raises an eyebrow.

"I do?"

"It's all over your face." I immediately see Wes in my head.

"So I'm told."

"That and you're like the loudest person in the hallway besides me," she adds.

I haven't talked to Wes since the evening I quit, not even when he called thirteen times, texted, and then showed up at my house. Luckily, that day I was out running at the track. I needed to move, jog—do anything but sit around hearing Wes in my head saying that I'm going to end up like my mother one day.

A small red light revolves in the rearview mirror. AAA pulls past and parks in front of Kylie's Corolla. I grab at the seat belt, readying to leave.

"Thank *god*," Kylie says, and I ignore the little voice in my head that tells me she wants nothing more than to get out of the car. She has her hand on the passenger door handle and gets out into the rain. I expect the slam of the car door, but instead she pops her head back in. "What are you doing tonight?"

"Me?"

"No. The other dope in the car."

I laugh. I've been wrong about Kylie—completely, *completely* wrong.

"I don't think I'm doing anything," I say even though I know I don't have plans. Wes and I probably would have gorged on popcorn at the movies or—wait, I forgot. It's the second night of the play.

"You need to come to a party with me," Kylie says. "I'll pick you up. Text me your address," she adds.

She reaches across the car to my cell sitting in a cup holder and types in her number.

She doesn't wait for me to say yes. She slams the door, runs to the woman getting out of the AAA van, and cries, "You're saving my life right now!"

The energy in my car is zinging. Kylie wants to take *me* to a party.

As I drive away, Kylie is jumping on the AAA mechanic. I don't need to sit inside alone. I don't have to explain myself to anyone. Kylie gets it. And I do need cheering up.

She is in the spotlight, not me. I can be the chorus and she can be the lead. That's perfect. Even if I'm not exactly sure what the parts will be or where I'm going to end up, with Kylie at the helm, I know with absolute certainty that it's going to be a wild ride.

PART TWO

Senior Year

September

FOUR

ONE OF THE BEST THINGS ABOUT KYLIE CASTELLI being my best friend is that she thinks I'm funny.

We're gathering our stuff at our lockers so we can haul ass after the last class of the day to the track for a quick run. I'm telling her my story about Alex James, party guy, and king of the Nantucket Red pants. Tank Anderson, who's as big as he sounds, pantsed Alex while Alex was *in the middle* of asking me out. He was inviting me to a concert and all of a sudden his pants were around his ankles, boxers and all. "I saw *everything.* And then he just threw the tennis ball in the air like it was *no big deal,*" I say. Kylie's crying, she's laughing so hard. Her long blond hair is pulled into a ponytail so her features are prominent, sharp.

When she laughs, her nose turns down slightly, and even then she's still so pretty. I play with my hair. It's long and brown with some touches of red, but it's still not as long as Kylie's. I've been growing it out since last summer.

Kylie has to hold herself up on the locker.

"He's . . . *endowed*," she says, wiping tears from her eyes. We make our way down the hall. "You won't ever be bored."

"Oh come on," I say. I don't mention that I've never had sex before, and Kylie's never asked. I let her think what she wants. In the year we've been friends, she hasn't pushed me to say anything I don't want to. It's one of her best attributes.

Kylie applies some lip gloss, and I feel a pang of jealousy that she can pull off such a bright, edgy color.

"You need to consider *someone*. You turn everyone down," she says.

"No, I don't."

"Okay, fine. You went on *one* date with that *one* guy from Prep who you met at the Joint." She means the live music club she drags me to nearly every Friday night.

She keeps going on and on about all of Alex's incredible attributes, but as she talks, a memory of a swirl of stars on a theater stage spins in my head. A memory I've never quite let go of. I pretend to flip through my planner as we walk to class.

"What's wrong?" Kylie asks. "Spill it."

"Bombed a quiz in pre-calc today. I didn't even study," I lie; I aced that test.

"You think I don't know when something is wrong," Kylie says, and a buzz of familiar anxiety whooshes through me at those words.

"What?" I laugh but it flutters. "Nothing is wrong."

"Uh-huh." But I know her tone. "It's annoying," she adds.

"Oh come on, Miss Ignorance Is Bliss," I counter. "I had to basically force you to tell me you had a crush on Tank."

"True, but I'm turning over a new leaf!" she says with a jump. "From now on I'm an open book."

Doubtful. Kylie's nearly as guarded as me—maybe even more so. She's the queen of deflecting.

"Oh shit, there's Lila!" she cries, and pulls us into the next hallway, out of eyeshot.

"What's the deal?" I ask, glancing back at Lila Suffolk and Eve Dennings. They are supposed to be our friends, but lately Kylie's been blowing them off whenever we have plans.

"Ugh. I'm so tired of Lila's copycat shit. And I told Eve about Tank asking me out last week and she proceeded to broadcast it to the whole world during lunch. You know how I am. I like my privacy."

We start walking again. I've seen Kylie do this before. She ices people out when they piss her off. Luckily, I get it. We're the same like that. Maybe it's why we became best friends so quickly.

But I can't help the little voice in my head. Usually Kylie doesn't pry but lately she's been asking me why Mom sleeps so much.

We pass a poster for the school play. It wasn't up earlier today so when we turn into the hallway toward English class, I make a point to see which play Ms. Taft has chosen. There's a huge photograph of a massive weeping willow tree. A full moon hangs over the tops of the fluffy branches. The words *And All Things*

Shall Be Peace are scrawled in cursive at the bottom of the page.

A Midsummer Night's Dream! Auditions September 28th!

Every single high school does *Midsummer.* Classic Taft. Shakespeare every two years—like clockwork. As we walk, even more people file in the hallway toward class. Kylie and I head away from the chaos of the main hallway and down another, which leads to the auditorium stage entrance. The drama club usually hangs out there, and I automatically look around for May, but I don't see her. I can't help but feel a little sad, thinking about the conversations May and I could have had about the wordplay and themes in *Midsummer* or the possible approaches that Taft could do. But I push that feeling away.

When I get to class, Ms. Reley is setting up a slide show with her computer. The only available seats are across the room from each other. Kylie, that loser, makes a beeline for the one near the window, knowing full well the other seat is next to Wes. I told her that Wes and I almost got together. She's kept a super fun tally of how many times he has said a full sentence to me since she and I became friends a year ago. We're up to nine.

When I glance at Kylie, she raises an eyebrow and opens up her notebook.

Wes is bent over his sketchbook. My first instinct is to ask him questions about *Midsummer.* Will it be a traditional performance? Modern day? Who designed the poster? He's hunched over his sketchbook, so I can't help but notice that his back and arms are more sculpted than they have ever been. I wonder if he'll try out for the part of one of the nobles or King Theseus. The old me would be trying out for Hermia or Helena, without a doubt.

Maybe I really *could* audition. Mom barely leaves her room these days, so I don't have to worry about her showing up. Since rehab, she doesn't drink anymore, but she's depressed all the time. Dad's been working on a piece for a carburetor in his basement shop for weeks. I'd just have to get past Taft's icy hatred of me.

I open my notebook and shake my head. I'm getting way ahead of myself. I left the acting life behind, and besides, I don't think it would exactly welcome me back with open arms.

Out of the corner of my eye, I see Wes's sketch. I recognize the layout for the stage. When Ms. Reley pulls down the projector screen and dims the lights, I lean over and whisper to Wes, "Set design?"

He keeps sketching and doesn't acknowledge that I've said a word. Not a shock. I probably shouldn't have said anything. I'm not even sure why I did.

"At least Taft is predictable—senior year, Shakespeare," I say, trying to fill his silence.

He pauses sketching; his pen hovers over a bird's-eye view of the auditorium and stage. "Yeah," he whispers.

He knows that I don't want to be strangers.

He glances up at the slide; it's of a painted depiction of Beowulf.

"I saw the meteor shower the other night," I say. "The one they keep playing on the news?" I've kept Wes's planetarium under my bed since last year, but I still like to look at the stars.

"Penny." He leans over to me. His warmth is familiar.

"Yeah," I say, waiting. My heart speeds up; he's *actually* going to say something?

"I'm not one of your dedicated followers," he whispers. "So don't bother."

The heat in my cheeks sears and I sit back in my chair.

I should have known this was pointless.

I spend the rest of class taking notes like a good English student. I don't dare to look over at Wes again—no matter how badly I want to.

"Freedom!" Kylie cries, and leaps from the double doors to the pavement. She's wearing an EG Private baseball hat and her hair flies in long blond braids. I throw mine into a long plait down my back. We head toward my car out on the senior parking lot. The air is so hot, it crackles with the threat of heat lightning.

Kylie is about to slide into the passenger seat when Tank's arm scoops her from the car and throws her around. She cries out, laughing between screams. I lower all the windows to let out the hot air and crank the AC.

"I'm not your rag doll!" she cries.

"Last Chance party tonight," Tank says once he places her down next to the passenger-side door.

"You've told me like ten times," Kylie says, and Tank nearly pushes Kylie in through the window, he's leaning toward her so hard. They haven't hooked up yet, but it's bound to happen. I love that moment. I almost had it with Wes—right before you get together with a guy. If you are normal, like Ky, then you actually end up getting together. If you're a moron, like me, you screw it up.

My phone chimes with text messages.

EVE: Homecoming nods are in.

LILA: You & Ky are nominated!

ME: I don't want to be nominated.

EVE: Too bad.

LILA: Get on board!

Homecoming nominations are kind of pointless. Anyone with a 3.1 GPA or higher can be nominated even if you only are nominated by one person. It's only if you get in the homecoming court that you could actually be voted queen or king.

As my phone continues to ding away, I glance up when Wes and May come out of school, followed by Panda and Richard. Panda lumbers in his familiar way, but I can't see what today's ironic T-shirt says. I could imagine Wes finding out about homecoming nominations. He would roll his eyes or grumble. But May . . . she might be different. I could see her being happy for me. She even talks to me sometimes in our US government class.

Panda lifts his hands in the air and makes claws with his fingers. He lumbers around Richard, May, and Wes in a circle, imitating a monster. His face is all screwed up and he's one of the funniest physical actors I know. He was Dogberry in *Much Ado*, one of my favorite characters. He launches himself on top of a car hood and I laugh, maybe too loud. May turns to me and my smile immediately falls. I lick my lips and frown at my lap as if she won't know I was laughing with my old group of friends.

I can't be all dodgy. I smile at her, tight-lipped, so I don't seem overeager. She returns it, which again, I suppose is a good thing, considering she ignored me this summer when she saw me at the Coffee Stop. Panda grabs May's attention when he does a dashing but oafish pirouette. May's smile widens, and she laughs, throwing her hair back. Her smile for Panda is real, not like the way she smiled for me.

"Ready, bitch?" Kylie says, and gets into the car.

"Your mouth is all red," I say about the apparently violent kissing that she engaged in with Tank. "Congratulations. Make-out session one accomplished."

"I'll be ready for session two tonight," she says with a whoop.

I look in the rearview at my old friends as I begin to pull away from the parking lot. Panda and May flip through the scripts for *Midsummer.* The ones that Taft is going to use for auditions. I make a point to rev the engine and peel out of the parking lot. They turn and look and I couldn't have timed it better—Kylie raises her arms in the air through the sunroof and with a high-pitched "whoo!" we descend down the long hill and away from school.

When I get home after a long run at the track, a savory mushroom gravy smell permeates the kitchen. Bettie left a potpie warming in the oven. She leaves on Fridays at four and I stopped waiting for Mom and Dad to eat dinner with me years ago. I drop my school and gym bags at the base of the kitchen table. My tank top sticks to my back and I turn the oven off just as my cell chimes.

KY: Pick me up at 9.

I'm slipping my phone back in my pocket when I see what's on the countertop next to the sink.

Two bottles of white wine. One is empty, the other halfway.

I draw a sharp breath and eye the Bellevue Rehab Facility

magnet on our fridge. It's not like it can help me, but it's there and somehow that comforts me. Dad must know. Maybe he's already called her doctor? Mom told us about the possibility of relapse, but she's been okay for a while now. I thought I saw a bottle of wine in her bedroom the other day, but when I went back to check it was gone. There weren't any in the sink.

A crash of glass echoes from downstairs in the basement.

"Damn it!" Dad bellows.

I sniff the air for sulfuric acid or any kind of burning. Nothing. Just the pie. He must be setting up for the carburetor. I slip the potpie out of the oven just as a few soft raps hit on the window behind me. It's too light to be a person knocking. Tiny bulbs of light pulse again and again—lightning bugs. Their tiny insect bodies tap, tap, tap as they fly into the glass. There's way more than I've seen before. And why are they out when it's still light out? Must be the humidity?

I grab a glass of water and step down into the basement, stopping at the door of Dad's shop. The main room is carpeted and still has my old toys in bins. A few couches sit before the TV. Dad's created some small metal parts that have gotten patented and sold to companies like Johnson & Johnson and John Deere. How Dad invented a part for a tractor, when he is from Providence, is beyond me. The house smelled like burning wires for months. I knock three times, my signal to Dad that I want to come in and can he please put away any acid or dangerous scientific mechanisms.

"Come in!" Dad calls.

His bald head reflects the work lights above. He has a wrench clenched between his teeth. Clear, thick goggles cover his glasses. This place never changes. My third-grade art is on the walls. All different types of saws, tools, and various plastic parts hang on pegboards. In the far back are stacked cans of paint and our old suitcases. We haven't gone on a family vacation in a long time. I motion to the various little pieces of metal organized in piles on the wooden worktable.

"What's this?" I ask. "For the carburetor?"

Dad goes on and on about mixing gasoline and air and the necessary channels, whatever that means. He mentions a Swiss engineering company that is interested in the design. In a lull in the conversation, I say, "There's wine at the sink."

He sighs and it's the kind where I know he has seen the wine too.

"Well, stay out of her way." He frowns at a metal piece that looks like a chicken nugget coated in silver.

"What are you going to do?" I ask.

Dad compares wrenches. He's never talked about what to do if Mom starts drinking the way she did before the rehab. I'm counting bottles again, which is never a good sign.

"What are we gonna do?" I press.

I wait for Dad to commiserate with me, but he focuses on finding the wrench for the chicken nugget thing. I'm not going to push it right now. No use going on about Mom until Dad actually *wants* to deal with it.

I just wish I knew how to save her from herself.

"So is that going to pay my college tuition?" I ask with a sigh.

"We'll see," he says. He's lost in thought.

He grabs a file and a tool I can't name but it looks like a handsaw. He sits down on the stool at the end of the table.

"Oh!" he says, clearly remembering something, and jumps up again to dig around in one of his many double-sided red toolboxes on a nearby shelf.

"I got nominated for homecoming queen," I say.

"That's great, Pen!" Dad says absently, still absorbed in whatever he's doing. Another few seconds go by, so I add, "College applications are coming up." I barely even raise my voice over the clanging from Dad's rummaging. He doesn't reply. "I'll probably go for small liberal arts, mostly. I have the Bates Common App pretty much ready to go. I'll need a—"

"There it is!" Dad cries. He pulls out what looks like a mini polisher.

No matter what it is, I've lost him. Done. Cooked. Even if I talk now, he's in the zone and won't reply unless I push, which could completely derail him. I know he needs this to distract himself from Mom. Maybe we both need to avoid the reality for a little while.

Within a few minutes, I'm back upstairs, my backpack is over my shoulder, and I have a plate filled with potpie.

I walk to the stairs to the sound of a saw buzzing in the basement. It's a purr when I get to the second floor. Mom is in her bedroom tinkering with her jewelry. The shades are drawn.

"Hey," I say, and place my food on the table outside her room.

Sometimes, when I catch her in a good mood, I can tell her about my life. But I never know when that will be. Even when she's sober, her depression makes it hard to talk to her sometimes.

Mom's delicate hands and the wisps of her black hair look so pretty by the soft light of the dresser lamp.

"Wow. That's pretty," I say, and pick up a dainty ring with a small blue gem. "Where did you get it?" I imagine myself in the pink dress I already bought for homecoming. I already wear another ring on my thumb. Kylie and I have the same one. It's silver with a blue circular stone. Mom's ring would look—

She snatches it from me. "You can't have it," she snaps. I back away and bring my hand to my stomach. It's like a hot string is pulled through my belly button. I didn't want the ring. I just wanted to talk.

I say nothing in return and leave her to organize her gold and gems. My mouth tugs downward. I slide my food silently from the table, walk up the stairs to my room, and close the door. I text Kylie.

ME: I'll grab the vodka. You grab the OJ for tonight.

FIVE

"THIS BAND IS SO GOOD!" KYLIE SAYS AS WE PULL up toward Tank's house. Rock music vibrates through my radio speakers. "I'm so obsessed!" Kylie cries, turning up the volume even more. Kylie has great taste in music. I have hundreds of songs and albums on my computer that I never would have heard in the first place if I hadn't become friends with Kylie. I instinctively glance at my backseat, where Eve and Lila would be sitting if Kylie wasn't "ghosting" them out of her life at present. They've been texting me instead, asking me what time we're going to the party. "Don't you just love this?" Kylie cries.

She waits for agreement from me, but I keep seeing those two damn wine bottles on the counter.

"What's up with you?" Kylie says. "You're being extra quiet." She pouts in the passenger mirror and applies lipstick. She lights a cigarette and when she takes a drag, the lipstick leaves a bright crimson ring around the end of her cigarette. I hate that she smokes in my car but I don't tell her to stop. Ky slips her cigarettes and green lighter into the front pouch of my purse.

"So, what did you say to Lila and Eve?" I say as we get out of the car. "So they wouldn't drive with us."

"That we ate dinner with your parents first."

I scroll through the texts from them. "They're obsessed with this homecoming nomination."

We get out of the car and when the music silences, I pretend to grab a microphone and interview Kylie. On cue, she jumps into Beauty Queen character. "Ms. Castelli," I say, "what will you do with your crown now that you are homecoming queen?"

"Well, first, I would make a point to change the . . ." She tries to search for what her duties as homecoming queen would be. "Shit," she says. "I don't want to have to do anything to be queen. I just want the pretty crown."

She smiles and we fall into laughter. I love Kylie's honesty.

"You totally get that interviewing thing from me," Kylie says, throwing her arm over my shoulder. "I'm your biggest influence. Radio DJ and all."

"Did you ever tell Mr. Pierce about the internship?" I ask. Kylie unhooks from my shoulder and pulls her hair out from its ponytail, tossing it around.

"I have an interview next month and Mr. Pierce is going insane that"—she makes air quotes—"one of his students will be working at a real radio station." She drops her hands. "Also, if I had to hear from you one more time," she says, and elbows me, "'If you don't try, Ky, you don't get!' I was going to wring your neck."

"It's true!" I cry.

"Yeah, yeah," she says with a smile.

Thick humidity has taken over the beginning of September. Even my rose perfume smells too sweet. Based on the number of cars in the driveway, it's a typical Friday-night party, which means that the usual suspects will be in attendance.

I wipe some sweat from my forehead as we walk up to the house.

"I wish we had a band for homecoming. Real musicians and not some stupid DJ," Kylie says as we head up to the house.

"Totally agree," I say. "Or you could DJ!"

"Now you're talking!" Kylie grins and loops her arm tightly in mine. "You're my number one, bitch!"

I squeeze her arm, which I always note is more muscular than May's, who has been small her whole life.

"This house is completely heinous," I say as we approach the steps.

Kylie cackles and her angled face shines under the moonlight.

No matter how many times I've been here, I still think Tank's house is tacky. Pillars abound. Mom would call it "ostentatious" and "trying too hard."

"You know Alex is going to ask you to homecoming," Kylie says. "Are you going to say yes?"

"If he can keep it in his pants," I reply, which sends her into laughter again.

"Tank hasn't asked me yet," Kylie groans. With the crystal chandelier hanging over the door, Kylie takes a second to preen in the reflection of the glass.

"He won't get a chance to ask you if we never go in," I say. "I could use a drink, you know."

"Miss One and Done?" Kylie says. "You think we don't notice but it's obvious."

I roll my eyes instead of fighting her on it. "Just because I don't kill the bottle like you do . . ."

It surprises me that Kylie notices that I don't really drink. I thought I hid it pretty well. I usually have one drink and that's it. There's no way I'm killing wine bottles like Mom. Either way, Kylie's been doing this a lot lately; telling me that I'm "holding out on her" or that we're not close when she's exactly like that—or she used to be. I've tried to blow it off, but these days it's making its way into all our conversations. She's told me a lot more about her mom and dad's divorce lately and how she feels whenever Tank is around. I don't want to reciprocate—not yet.

Kylie tosses her hair around in the reflection of the house door before opening it up to the loud noise of the party inside. I notice, even though it wasn't intentional, that our black dresses are nearly identical. Tonight is probably the last time we'll be able to wear these minis until next summer.

"Hot during the day then cold at night. Or then so hot that our faces melt off. This weather is bipolar," Kylie says.

"I know, I keep thinking it's cute boots weather, but it was what? Eighty today?" I ask.

People love to throw around terms like "bipolar," "manic," and "depressed." They don't know what it's like to live with someone who sleeps in a dark room all day and hardly emerges unless she's drunk. Or what it means when your mother tells you not to touch her things.

She can have whatever she wants of mine.

The music is booming and Kylie and I fall into the party just as the best hip-hop song bounces through the sound system. I couldn't have timed it better myself. Kylie and I swing our hips to the beat. The hallway to the living room is our catwalk.

"Hello!" I cry out to the crowd when we step into the foyer. I spin in the center of the room with a bottle of vodka in my hands.

"Penny!" People call my name from different corners of the room. I take a deep breath and recite a monologue from the play *Willow Street.* It won an Obie, a Laurence Olivier Award, and a Tony last year. No one here knows that, though. They think I'm just being funny. Kylie's funny sidekick.

"Well, well." I bring my hand to my chest. I channel the lead of Carrie Isner, the rich Southern girl who loves elegant parties more than life itself. "Look at all these beautiful people. All the gorgeous smiles and happy faces. Did you ice the cake? Chill the drinks? I have just what you asked for. . . ." I lift the bottle into the air and the applause echoes around me. I bow.

"You could be famous!" someone calls out from a group of girls that I occasionally sit with at lunch.

"You're really good," a girl named Erica says.

"Thanks, Erica," I say with a smile and a casual wave of my

hand. She stands a little straighter because I know her name—she thinks she knows me. No one really does. I still read plays when they get a good review in the *New York Times* and I watch all the award shows. They think I'm just loud, funny Penny, top ten in the class and the party girl at Kylie's side who never takes anything too seriously.

We move into the kitchen, I place the bottle on the counter, and Kylie throws an arm over my shoulder. "What is Wes doing here?" she says in my ear.

I accidentally knock a cup of limes aside. They fall to the floor and I scramble to pick them up. *Please don't let him come in the kitchen. Just give me a minute.* I need to act normal.

"What the hell is he doing here?" I whisper when I stand back up.

"I think he came with Panda."

I've seen Panda at parties but haven't hung out with him one-on-one in a while. He's good for weed, so he's always invited. Since I don't smoke, it hasn't led to us talking that much.

When I stand up, I peer through the people dancing and a group of guys playing cards. Tank comes into the house from outside. Wes follows next with Panda but has to hunch a bit because he's too tall for the doorway. Adrenaline shoots through my chest. I turn my back to the living room and start to make a drink. Kylie is reluctantly called away by Lila and Eve and I've just finished making her drink when the scent of salt-and-vinegar potato chips wafts over to me.

"What's up, Panda?" I say, but my voice is wobbly. When I face him, I expect to see Wes too but Panda's alone.

He pulls at the fabric of his T-shirt, right at the stomach area, as he always does. Today's T-shirt has a picture of a wolf howling at the moon.

"The famous Penny Berne screwdriver?" he asks instead, and tips his chin to my drink.

"Shall I make you a beverage?" I ask, gesturing to the orange juice.

"Nah," Panda says. "Coca-Cola." He lifts his cup. "My mom is on my ass about alcohol."

I'm surprised he's so open talking to me about his family since that incident happened back in May. I was coming home from the track and Panda and his dad were stuck at the long red light at the corner of Green and Main. I recognized the blue Mercedes. He was *screaming* at Panda. I stopped in the next lane and could hear Panda's dad through the open sunroof. Panda's chin was to his chest and when the light turned green, his dad sped forward to the parking lot at the bottom of the hill to school. His dad slammed the door and I sat at the light watching Panda get reamed. His cheeks were bright red and old tears stained his face.

Jamie, you make my life difficult! Do you ever do anything you say you're going to do? Why do I pay for that school?!

It was so weird to hear Panda called by his real name, Jamie, as I never ever hear it except in theater reviews or in official class documents. He's always just been Panda.

That day, I knew he was due to set up for *Into the Woods* rehearsal. His father yanked at the duffel bag in Panda's hand. He raised his hand high above his head. I swear he was making a fist. I revved the engine, sped to the parking lot, and screeched on the brakes, slamming the car door behind me as I got out.

"Hey!" I yelled, pointing at Mr. Thomas. He was all out of breath. "You'll hurt him, Mr. Thomas! Don't!" Mr. Thomas opened his mouth, but closed it. I think he did it a couple of times before he got into the car, leaving Panda in the parking lot. That made sense, as I am sure he was driving Panda to rehearsal, but I don't know what could have made him scream at Panda so violently. The Mercedes tires screeched as he sped off. I was all out of breath and flushed when I turned to Panda. He nodded without making eye contact with me. His eyelashes were thick with tears.

"Panda," I croaked.

"You're a good egg, Berne," he said. "You're good."

And he walked up the hill toward school without ever bringing it up again—until now.

Kylie's laughter rises over the music, bringing me back to the kitchen at Tank's house. She says something to Tank and presses her hand against his chest. I would like to ask Panda what part he thinks he wants in *Midsummer*—but I don't. I never did find out what his dad was yelling at him about that day.

"That's a serious shirt for a night such as this," I say, gesturing to Panda's T-shirt.

"Don't fuck with the wolf," Panda replies, and sips on his Coke. "I miss you, Berne," he says.

I want to ask Panda why I haven't seen him at parties since last spring, and why he skipped being in an Ocean State Theater Company play this past summer. I follow the play schedule and privately scrutinize who is starring in the summer productions. I didn't see his name once and I know he's been in OSTC since he was eight. Just like May and me.

"How come I didn't see you in any of my classes?" I ask. We were in three together last year.

Panda sips on his Coke. "I'm not in senior classes this year."

That doesn't make sense. "Why not? You were in *both* my AP classes last year."

He doesn't answer because the bass bumps up a bit and members of the basketball team come into the kitchen. Tank leads the way. We both know that the guys on the basketball team can pick on Panda, but they never let it go too far. He gets the good weed and can fix their computers better than any tech guys at school. He scoots out undetected and I get why he wants out of the room. Kylie comes back by my side at the sight of Tank. I don't know how to be when she needs me to be the one in the spotlight.

"We heard a girl in here makes a really good screw," Tank says with his familiar booming voice. I cannot understand why guys have to make fun of a girl in order to interact with her.

"Yes, I will make you a drink," I say with a roll of my eyes. "Hand me your cup."

Tank hugs me to him with a shoulder squeeze.

I make some drinks for Tank and the guys and pass them out—the vodka bottle is nearly empty. It doesn't matter how many anyone thinks I had, even though I hardly ever drink.

"To Penny!" Tank cries. Seven players on the basketball team stand around me and raise up their red cups.

"To Penny!" they echo.

I curtsy.

"Tank looks so good," Kylie whispers in my ear. I nudge her with my elbow.

She bites at her nails.

"What if it's just a hookup?" she says.

Beyond Kylie, out in the living room, I see Wes pass by. I miss my friend so much, it nearly physically aches.

I angle my body to lean against the wall for a better view. My heart pounds in my throat. I can't help it—it's like a magnetic pull now that Wes is in the room. Wes pushes his blond hair out of his eyes and readjusts his knit beanie. A thin leather strap wraps tight around his neck. That's new. He finally catches me watching him. My stomach dips. He's in a formfitting gray T-shirt. Sparks erupt in me, deep in the center of my belly—not butterflies, but a fire. I want to touch him, even just to see what his skin feels like now. But I pushed him away, and I can never have him back. That part of my life is over.

"How do I look?" Kylie flattens out the front of her dress and applies more red lipstick.

"Great," I say, but it's a reflex.

"God, Penny, act a little bit *less* interested," she snaps at me.

"I *am* interested. Come on, Ky. You guys kissed today. Tank is yours."

"Like it's so easy?" She sighs. "Go talk to Wes. You stare at him all day."

I clench.

"No, I don't," I whisper.

"Yes. You do. You rejected him, and you regret it." I hate that she's raising her voice.

I check to see if anyone can hear Kylie outside of the kitchen. "Shh," I say.

"No!" she cries. "I can't take it anymore! You think I'm stupid, that I don't notice." She points at the center of her chest. "I'm your best friend. I notice!"

Her words are little barbs tangling up in my head. I don't know how to move around them, I don't know how to pull them loose. She's supposed to be safe—the one I can go to when I don't want to think about the things that hurt.

Tank and the guys are pretending not to listen but Kylie isn't good at subtle.

"I'm sorry," she continues. "It's infuriating. If you would just share *something.* Like once in a while . . ."

"I do tell you," I say weakly. "Everything."

She laughs. "Okay, Penny," she says, and the sarcasm is typical Kylie. "You always want to come to my house, for one," she says. "You never invite me to yours."

My heart beats high in my chest. How could she just say this in front of everyone? Lila and Eve stand by Alex James, trying not to look obvious that they're listening.

"My house sucks," I say before she can list off anything else. "Yours is way better for hanging out. And my mom—"

"Your mom is in her pajamas all the time. Who cares?" she snaps. Her jaw drops and I can tell she wants to apologize instantly after she says it. But a hot anger rips through me.

Now everyone knows that my home life is shit.

"Coming from you this sounds ridiculous, Ky. You blew off Lila and Eve because they are—what were the words you said? Copycats? Or because Eve broadcasted that you like Tank? I'm not the only one who keeps secrets."

I turn to walk away, get some air outside, and cool off. I shouldn't have yelled at her.

Kylie pulls me back on my shoulder. I yank out of her grasp.

"Oh, so you're just going to walk away?"

"You're a hypocrite," I say, and I know how tinny and small it sounds. I'm sweating and there are too many eyes on me.

"Maybe I am," Kylie snarls. She sips on her drink. "But I've got news for you, Penny Berne. So are you."

The music is playing but our conversation might as well be pumped out on a loudspeaker.

Heat rushes through me.

I snatch the bottle of vodka from the counter and blow past Wes and Panda, who stand next to the open patio door. With my bottle in hand, I tear past them and move from the patio down the stairs toward the swimming pool below. Kylie, Lila, Eve, and some of the guys on the basketball team follow behind, but I keep going.

"She's just drunk!" Lila's voice echoes behind me. She catches up to me when I get down to the pool. I take a heavy drink from the vodka bottle and pass it to Lila. The bitter taste is surprising—I never drink it straight, it's always mixed with lots of juice. I hide my grimace by turning away from Lila and Eve. At the pool table and chairs, I kick off my shoes. People are getting out of the water but a couple of girls are still in the hot tub. Thunder crackles in the sky. A trickle of sweat runs down my back. Even the smoke from the cigarettes in the air is warm and sour.

"What are you doing, Penny?" Kylie says, coming down to the pool. The air around us glows with lightning bugs. "Come on, stop. It's going to rain soon."

"Damn lightning bugs," I say without answering Kylie, and smack one away with the back of my hand. I keep my eyes on the zigzagging movements of the lightning bugs but they blur around me, from the heat or the vodka or both. Beer bottles and cigarette smoke litter the ground and air. A rap song plays from the house and echoes out into the night.

I want to be in the pool under the water where I can't see Kylie or Wes. My back is tight, my neck too. I rub at my eyes.

A girl I know from bio class is wrapped in a towel and wringing out her hair next to the hot tub, which is now empty. The ground is still warm from the scorching eighty-degree day. I stand at the rim of the pool and curl my toes over the edge. The humidity is so thick that thin wisps of mist hover and twist into the air.

The bass from the party music reverberates over the water.

I spin to the crowd on the second-floor landing.

"Who wants a drink?" I say, and note that Kylie has her arms crossed over her chest, but I draw in a sharp breath when I see there is sympathy in her eyes. Or maybe it's not sympathy—maybe it's pity. I lift the bottle to the sky as a round of cheers echoes from Tank and the guys.

A signature move for a signature drink.

I drain the last sips and pass the bottle off to Lila.

Then I jump.

The water swallows me whole. I expect people to jump in with me. Any minute, bodies will plunge into the depths of the pool. As I descend the pressure builds and water envelops my body.

I hug my arms close, but my back pulls up and I float toward the surface. I can't stay on the bottom of this pool without a fight.

My body rises and my chest constricts. My lungs are starting to demand air. I break the surface and flip my hair backward. I blink the water out of my eyes and tiny pelts of rain hit my nose.

"Hey, where is every—"

A downpour smacks the patio tiles and people scramble up the stairs back to the house. Tank and a couple of the other guys on the terrace above call down to me. Tank shakes his head with a smile. Eve uses her jacket to shield her hair and scurries up to the main patio.

"Come on!" Lila cries. Her heels clomp as she runs up the first few stairs. People from various landings call my name. I don't see Kylie.

My hands cut through the water, stroke after stroke. I'm almost at the ladder. I duck underwater, outstretch my fingers to the smooth metal handle. I lift my right leg and the bottom of my foot touches the deepest step.

Bright blast.

Hot light. It's all I can see.

Fractured, fragmented, thousands of slices of white-and-blue light.

The pool water is burning.

Try to kick, Penny.

My legs are anchors pulling me to the bottom.

"Penny! Oh my god! Someone call an ambulance!" Lila shrieks. There's a rip in her voice.

The sound bleeds.

My leg muscles clench and radiate. Every part of me is burning. Someone cool my arms, they're burning. My legs are burning. I'm in the water but I'm on fire.

I try to breathe but my chest is frozen.

What's happening to me?

I choke and gag.

People are screaming. Their shrill pitch pierces the water.

It fills me, like the water in my lungs, like the weight of my arms and legs.

The yelling and the heat and the light push me farther to the bottom of the pool. Lower and lower, until there is no more light. Only darkness.

And silence.

SIX

THE LIGHT IS CRACKED AND YELLOW.

I need to close my eyes.

Call a fucking ambulance! She's not breathing.

"Penny, can you hear me?"

"I don't think she's responsive."

"IV stat."

Beeping. Something's beeping.

White-tiled ceiling.

Where am I?

I want to swallow but I can't.

"Penny. Penny. It's okay." It's Dad's voice. Dad. Dad is here.

"Get back. Get back." A female voice. Something hard is in

my throat. Plastic. I'm choking. I'm choking but I'm not underwater. Something blocks my throat. *Dad, help me!*

Heat shoots through my arm, through my veins.

A nurse points at me. Red fingernail polish—like blood.

"She's coming out . . ." a deep voice says. The sound is unbalanced. Strong at first then it fades. "Penny? Please stand back. Stand back." The voice moves away from me.

"Penny . . . can you hear me?" Dad's voice.

My eyelashes shield my eyes from the light so it can't come all the way through. I want to see Dad. My right foot is fat and swollen. I want someone to rest ice on my foot.

"Penny, I love you. You're okay. It's Dad."

I blink away the fractured canary light. Dad drifts into view. The top of his bald head is shiny.

"Penny. I want you to nod if you can hear me," Dad says.

"Vitals look good." There is the deep voice again, fading away.

It is not Wes's deep voice. Where is Wes? I just saw him. Didn't I?

"Heart rate normal," Deep Voice says.

"Penny—" Dad.

Clear sound.

"Nod if you—"

Clearish.

"Can hear me . . ."

Like there's a shell over my ear.

I raise my chin a little up and down. My neck is so stiff. My cheeks are tight.

"That's good, Penny Pen," Dad says. "Real good."

Someone's squeezing my fingers. I turn my head and when I do, an accordion unfolds in my neck. Mom stands by the bed and holds my fingers in hers.

"M—" I try to push sounds out of my mouth. "M—" Something blocks them.

She wears a pink sweater.

Beyond her, the sunset drips down a high-rise building. Mom is backlit in tangerine. The light bleeds from the glass to her sweater. She rests her hand on my arm and I reach to lay my fingers over hers.

There's a tug on my skin. I squint.

An IV digs into the top of my hand.

Mom sits down next to me, drawing half the weight of the bed toward her. I press down on the sheets. With a *bolt* there is a sharp pain, deep in the center of my palm.

I cry out, hunching over. I can't make it stop. It radiates, it needles. My fingers are stuck straight—too straight. I want to curl them but can't.

Like a wrench. Like a vise. The middle of my palm pulses.

Deep Voice is next to me talking very fast, but I don't know what he's saying. Someone applies pressure to my fingers, prying them apart.

"Is that a seizure?" Dad asks. "Is she having a seizure?"

The strong hands keep pushing against my fingers. Pain tears through me. The muscles in my hand pulse, again and again, until—finally—they release.

I collapse back down on the bed. I didn't even know I was

sitting up until the muscles in my back unclench.

Mom wipes some sweat from my forehead. Her fingertips are soft.

"Well, is it?" Dad asks. "Some kind of seizure?"

"No," Deep Voice says. A doctor? He's wearing a white coat that says *Abrams*, but my vision is blurry and smeared and I lose focus. I blink hard. The doctor bends down to the side of the bed and, after meeting my eyes, he looks to the ceiling.

"Can you switch the light off?" he calls to someone.

The brightness of the room falls to a muted orange light. The name on his coat shifts into focus, and now I can clearly see the dark cursive stitched onto the pocket. *Neurology Resident.*

"Penny." Dr. Abrams speaks in an even tone. "You're in Providence Memorial. You were struck by lightning two days ago. Your left side was hit. I know it sounds opposite, but where you were hit seems to be affecting your right hand. The spasm you experienced in your right hand is because your brain is sending too many signals to your hand. It should equalize soon."

He's talking too fast. Struck by lightning? Providence Memorial? Brain signals?

I'm in the hospital?

"Where is she?" a new voice says.

That voice. I know that voice. It's a girl's. I try to place her but I can't.

"You have to let me see her! I was the one who saw her in the pool, damn it!" the girl cries. A jolt of adrenaline rushes through my chest. *How* do I know her?

"I'm sorry, miss, your friend was struck by lightning. She

needs rest, she can't see visitors yet." My neck creaks. She is my friend. This girl is my friend.

It has to be May, my *best* friend, but it doesn't sound like her. The voice sounds different, higher.

"It's just immediate family today, you can come tomorrow."

My mind is racing. *Lightning?*

"L . . ." is what I get out. Was I in a pool? Whose pool was I in? I try to remember where I was last. *Where* was I last? As the girl walks away, I hear the click of her heels. I want her to come back, but she is gone.

I don't remember what she's talking about. I don't remember anything. I try. My head hurts from trying.

There was a *Much Ado About Nothing* rehearsal; it was a warm day in May and everyone was annoyed about having to wear those heavy costumes when it was so hot. Bettie had called and said I needed to come home right after rehearsal. I must have ignored her and gone swimming in May's pool. That must have been where I got struck.

I should remember what happened. But I can't.

"Penny, did you hear the doctor?" Dad says. "You were struck by lightning."

"Wh—" I croak. The word "where" is there on the tip of my tongue but it burns in my throat. I keep my eyes on Mom's black bob, instead. It's longer than I remember and reaches past her chin. Did it grow and I haven't noticed? I have been super busy with rehearsals for *Much Ado*. I reach my fingers up again toward her face. My left hand shakes and my arm is too tired.

She thinks I am reaching for water so she hands me the cup and wraps her fingers around mine to help me hold it to my lips. My hand shakes. Water dribbles down my chin. I sip and it is nearly the best thing I have ever had as it trickles down my searing throat. Dad presses a button, lifting the bed so I'm sitting up.

The nurse shuts the door and Dr. Abrams takes my hand in his; he's warm. "I am going to show you something. I know your sight might be a little weak," he says. Beyond him, the sunset is a smear reflected in the glass high-rise building.

"Penny? Can you hear the doctor? Are you listening?" Mom asks.

Dr. Abrams is tall and has lots of hair that shoots up in white-blond spikes.

"I want you to look at my eyes," he says. I don't want to look away from Mom's face but the doctor lifts a handheld mirror up and, weirdly, holds it over my forearm so it reflects my skin. I squint.

Then my eyes focus, and I see myself.

Vines. There is no other word for what I see. Golden branches spread across my skin like tangled brambles. I expect full flower buds to be at the end, but the branches are like ivy that crawls over buildings, except this ivy is copper. The thin designs etch up and down my thigh, along my shin, and stop at the top of my foot. Dr. Abrams runs his index finger down the length of my arm without touching me.

"We think the lightning left your body at your feet. According to your friends who spoke to the EMTs, you were on the ladder trying to climb out of the pool. It conducted the lightning and blew you back in."

My heart slams and I hear the powerful beats in my head.

"What—what—" My breath comes out in puffs. I'm too hot. I push off the blanket and the cool air-conditioning feels better on my legs. I clutch the fabric but need to release it immediately because my hands are shaking.

"I know it's overwhelming," the doctor says. His voice echoes around the room. My ears feel funny. "Penny, I want you to say a sentence. I know it will be hard. But I want you to say a full sentence—*any* sentence."

"W-Wi—"

I grimace. Say it. Form the words.

"W—will . . ." I exhale. My lips, like my cheeks, feel swollen and hard. "Will I . . . be-be . . . okay?" I finally say.

Mom wipes away a tear. Dad lowers his head and turns away toward the door. Dr. Abrams's eyes wrinkle at the corners when he smiles.

"Your motor skills will return. And that sentence," the doctor speaks softly, "was a real test. To see where we are at with your speech. It'll only get better as the days go on."

I'm not sure how he can say that when vines scrawl all over me.

"These are called Lichtenberg figures," he explains when he sees my gaze go back to the designs. "The leafy, plant-like markings will fade in a few days."

The branches spread over my forearms, up to my biceps and shoulders. They stop near my neck.

"You're actually quite lucky," the doctor says. "Some people have them on their face. But then again, those people don't usually live to tell the tale."

Another doctor, tall with a shock of red hair, takes photographs of my arms. I blink away the spots of light from the flash, but the bright light burns on the backs of my eyelids.

"Put that away," Mom snaps at the resident. "It hurts her eyes."

"W-w-wha-what are they?" I ask.

"Essentially, they're much like bruises," Dr. Abrams explains. "They generally fade in a few hours, sometimes days. We have seen some cases of them lasting months; we call that tattooing. Either way, they *will* go away." With a light pat on my hand, the doctor turns to the nurse.

"Let's get a CBC, baseline blood work, then let's get some real food into her," Dr. Abrams says.

"Mom?" I get out through stutters. "Was that—" I have to take a breath. "M-m-m-May at the door?"

Mom's eyebrows draw together.

"May?" she says, and there's something in her tone that makes me nervous.

I really try hard not to stutter. "May," I say again to clarify.

Dr. Abrams says something quickly to Mom. He keeps his back to me so the sound is uneven and I can't work out what he's saying.

"No, honey, that was Kylie." She nods at me and smiles to be encouraging.

Kylie. I don't know a Kylie. Do I?

I must frown because Mom sits down on the edge of the bed.

"Your friend Kylie—" Mom looks to Dad. "What's her last name?"

"Casseni? Castelli? Or something like that," Dad replies. This conversation is moving too fast.

"But, M-Ma-May," I say again.

"You and May haven't been friends for a while. Kylie is your best friend now," Mom explains. "It's been you and Kylie for a year or so now."

I don't understand. My mouth tastes bitter and I want to grip the blanket again but my hands are too weak. I squeeze my eyes shut. I want my friends to be here. I want Wes, Karen, May, and Panda. Why don't I know what anyone is talking about?

Dad sits down on the other side of the bed next to me. I focus on his glasses. The frames are thick plastic, different from his usual wire rims.

"When did you c—ch-change your glasses?" I ask. Dad looks back at the doctor and then at me. He usually has a glimmer of mischief in his eye, but right now there's nothing.

"Penny, what day is it?" Dad asks. I don't like this. I search my memory. Of course I know what day it is. Tech week was starting on that Saturday so Taft was completely on edge. The doctor said it had been two days since the strike.

"Monday?"

"What month?" Dad asks.

The bed is hard. I don't like the bright light of the sunset in the corner of my eye. I need more space. It's May. I know it's May but I don't want to say it out loud. I don't like the way they're all staring at me, like there's something wrong.

"Penny, can you answer your dad?" Dr. Abrams says.

"Ma-May," I say. "Tech w-w-eek."

"Tech week?" Mom whispers to Dad.

"It's September eighteenth, Penny," Dr. Abrams says slowly.

Out of the corner of my eye, I see a newspaper on the windowsill. I stretch out my hand and Mom gets approval from Dr. Abrams before handing it to me. He nods once and Mom gives me the newspaper. With vibrating fingers, I pull it closer to my eyes.

September 18th, 2016.

I grip the paper and bring it close to my face. The black letters are blurry. I need to squint.

2016. I rub at my eyes with the back of my hand so the IV scratches at my eyebrows.

2016 . . .

2016 . . .

2016 . . .

I can't move. Someone is pressing on my legs to keep me in the bed. I try and try to move.

"We're going to need some help in here!" the red-haired doctor yells.

Why do they need to keep me here? I'm deep in a black cavern and I want to crawl out. I am screaming, the vocal cords strain.

It's been *more* than a year.

Mom brings her face close to mine.

"Penny, it's okay. We'll explain. Everything will make sense."

Her hard fingers grip my burns shaped like vines. Heat rushes through my veins.

2016.

I don't remember the past year.

I don't remember any of it.

SEVEN

DAY ONE:

Here's what I know:

The year is 2016.

I have no memory from May 2015 through today, September 18th, 2016.

In the hospital, my legs shake when they make me walk so they give me a shiny wheelchair. I want to be sitting on my bed at home with May. I want Panda to come over with potato chips and tell me about Taft's insanity.

I missed Christmas. I missed Panda's New Year's party. I missed *Much Ado About Nothing*.

I want to see Wes so much that I curl up tight in the hospital bed.

DAY TWO

The walker they give me has tennis balls on the feet.

"Push, shuffle, push, shuffle," the nurse tells me.

The numbness in my right foot makes it more like: Push, drag. Push, drag.

When I'm back in bed, I slip under the covers so the sheet is over my head. I don't care that I look like I'm five. I can't stop thinking about Wes and I want him to just pick up the phone and explain why he isn't here harassing the nurses to see me. Why isn't he here with Panda making jokes at the side of my bed? I hold the hospital phone close to my ear and dial. First ring, I hold my breath. Second and third, I silently beg that he'll pick up—and at the fourth ring his voice mail picks up. "It's Wes. Leave a message. Make it quick."

His voice is deeper. It was deep the last time we spoke but this is smooth. Like a—it's weird to even think it. Like a man. It knocks me off my game and I stumble over my words once the phone beeps.

"Um, hi. It's Penny. I guess you heard about the lightning. I'll be out in a couple of days. Anyway, I'm rambling so if you could call me back at the hospital that would be good. I have some questions. I—" My voice catches in my throat and I wince. "I just have some questions about what's been going on. I don't have my cell, it was damaged in the pool. So, um. Just call me back, okay?"

I hang up and after a moment of holding my breath, I groan, wishing I had never called.

DAY THREE:

Push, drag. Push, drag. Push, drag. Push, drag.

I miss running at the track with Wes on weekends. I miss the lemon water and the fights over what music we would listen to. I miss running eight-minute miles and leaving him far behind, panting, with his hands on his thighs.

Push, drag. Push, drag. Push, drag. Push, drag. Push, drag. Push, drag . . .

Why hasn't he called me back?

DAY FOUR:

They move me to crutches when I'm feeling brave. I fall a few times—my bones rattle. It aches in the center of my chest, directly between my lungs. Every time I think of my friends and every time I stare at that hospital phone, it throbs.

"It could be worse," the nurse says, trying to be nice. "What if you lost all your memory?"

My kneecaps are purple from falling.

There are more and more tests. Whether it's in a bed or a chair, I am transported everywhere on wheels. At one appointment, they place sticky dots on my chest—an EKG. Effects can come later, they say.

Much later.

During a brain scan they give me cold lemonade for the metallic taste that has been lingering in my mouth since I woke up. It makes me think of the frozen lemonade from this summer—or, I guess, last summer—when Panda, Wes, May, and I sat on the town dock watching the Welcome Summer Festival fireworks.

I want to get in touch with people but the doctors won't let me look at a computer screen. Dr. Abrams thinks the brightness of the screen could cause a seizure or a hand spasm.

So I let it go.

DAY FIVE:

When I come back from physical therapy I ask the nurse if there are any calls for me. I even ask the nurses at the main station, but they tell me that the "phone hasn't rung once." I scan the room, looking at the cards and flowers and notes from family. I wonder if Mom packed away the important ones from my friends or took them home as I'll be leaving in a day or two. I don't see Wes's block lettering or May's loopy cursive anywhere. I don't open any cards with handwriting I don't recognize. I drop them into my duffel bag.

Wes must be at rehearsal or working on some new contraption like the tree Taft wanted him to cut out of wood for *Much Ado*. Maybe he's crafting something for my messed-up brain.

He'll show up. He will.

DAY SIX:

"The uneven weather has caused a surge of the lightning bug population. We're here at Stevenson Park at dusk to see the array of lights. Really, it's much more like a show here this evening." The

Channel Six journalist with a severe blond bob stands before the lush green trees of the state park. Even at dusk, tiny lights pop in and out of the evergreen trees. I'm sitting in the physical therapy room before being discharged, waiting to see Dr. Abrams. Mom is on her way to pick me up and this is the last "hurdle" before I am officially let out. But right now, I don't know how to feel about going back to my regular life.

Last night, Dad told me I quit theater back in the summer after tenth grade. I say the four words over and over. *I quit the theater.* I wasn't even in *Much Ado.* I don't know who played Beatrice. It makes so much more sense that Wes and May aren't returning my calls. They must be so mad at me.

How could I quit theater?

I take a sip of lemonade, the third glass I have had today. The taste of metal coats my mouth. It's acrid, bitter. To wash it away they've been giving me sweets, sucking candies, juice, and popsicles.

It will fade, they tell me. But when?

"Aren't these just unnatural beauties!?" an expert coos from the TV.

"Though I do have to mention," the blond journalist says to the expert, *"it seems that they may be growing in numbers. Do you have any thoughts on this?"*

Dr. Abrams walks into the room with an oversize manila envelope and clipboard. A clipboard means new information.

"Let's go sit," he says, and motions to the cubicle at the back of the room.

I limp slowly toward the cubicle, pressing my foot against

the floor, but it feels the same as it has all week—fat, numb, and uneven. I sit down with Dr. Abrams behind the pink plasterboard.

"This is a list of your team of doctors. As you know, I'm your neuro specialist, then you have the counselor—"

"Counselor?" I say.

"It's important you talk to someone about how you're feeling, even if you go to someone at your school."

I nod and tell him I've already talked to the hospital therapist, but Dr. Abrams raises an eyebrow. He sits back, pulling the list of doctors away.

"I heard you've been waiting to hear from some friends."

I look at the desk and walls of the cubicle.

"I guess they're busy," I whisper. "I wouldn't even know what to say if they did show up. It's been a long time."

I expect Dr. Abrams to refer me to the counselor again but he considers me and says, "What would you want to say?"

"That there must be a reason I quit theater. I want to know why."

"Is that connected to the last memory you have?" Dr. Abrams asks.

"I think so."

He sighs. "Well, people have been known to purposefully block things out."

"Why?"

"It's too hard for them to think about a specific memory or deal with a situation emotionally."

"I guess it doesn't really matter, does it? I'm here, aren't I?

Sitting at this ridiculous pink cubicle, and I have to start over."

"What would make you happy right now?"

"If everything didn't taste like metal. That would make me happy."

He smiles. "Besides the obvious, I mean." He takes some notes and chuckles.

"What?" I say.

"You remind me of my daughter."

"You have a daughter?" I say quietly.

"She's a little younger than you. She's always moaning and groaning when I ask her to talk about something going on in her life."

"I wish my dad would want to spend time with me at all." The words just fly out into the air between us in that pink cubicle. I didn't even know they were true until just now.

Dr. Abrams says nothing, but presses his lips together. I clear my throat, nodding to the clipboard and manila envelopes resting on the bubble-gum-colored desk. He goes through the rest of the doctors I'll get to know over the next few months and then lays out a set of MRIs images as well as what I assume to be the EKG report.

"Your mom is on her way here, but I've got a surgery soon and have her permission to tell you your newest test results."

A flutter high in my chest makes my breath short.

"Are they bad?"

"They explain a lot. But nothing we didn't expect."

"Oh," I say in a huge exhale, and my back hunches over a bit. I hadn't realized I had been sitting so straight.

He points to one of the MRIs of my brain.

"As we saw from the initial MRIs at the beginning of the week, neurological complications are very common following a lightning strike. We don't see any major damage to the frontal lobe but—" He stops and points at three white spots on the scan of my brain. "These are small lesions, which may be causing the spasms in your hand and your memory loss."

"What is a lesion exactly?"

"When there's someone with damage from trauma or who suffers from recurrent migraines, a lesion can present itself on a scan. It's like a small injury to your brain, a signal that there is a little damage. Sometimes it's just a temporary spot we need to watch. For you, we think it's linked to your acute memory loss."

My lesions don't seem like much more than three white specks.

"We're going to monitor you, see how you do when you get back to school. That way we can track when your memory comes back."

I lift my eyes to Dr. Abrams and his spiky white hair. "When it comes back?"

The hope of this makes tears bite at my eyes and I swallow hard, concentrating so I don't lose it completely.

"With some neuro therapy, yes, some memories should resurface. But there's no guarantee." Dr. Abrams stands up and I do too, pushing my chair back into the cubicle. I let my left hand linger on the chair back. Mainly because it's so cool from the icy air-conditioning.

"We're going to do everything we can. Every lightning strike victim is different." He hands me a stack of pamphlets and print-outs. "Read through this information, it may help you to adjust. And remember, no screen time for another week or so, to give your eyes enough time to recover."

"Thanks," I say, and look down at the papers in my hands. The top page has a bunch of strike victim testimonies, and the one after that has information about online communities for survivors.

"Let's be optimistic about this," Dr. Abrams says. "I know it's scary and frustrating, but you were very lucky, Penny." He tucks his clipboard under his arm. "So let's focus on that for now."

EIGHT

MY FIRST NIGHT AT HOME, DINNER IS "WHATEVER I want," which ends up being takeout from Pals, the best Italian restaurant in East Greenwich. The kitchen is the same as the last time I saw it, which is comforting. Except Mom has new designer plates. These ones have tiny sprigs of rosemary that circle the rims.

There's rosemary, that's for remembrance. Pray you, love, remember.

Ugh, of course I can recall a line from *Hamlet* with no problem, but the last year of my life? Nope.

Mom and Dad have given me a new cell phone, and it charges on a chair near the table while we eat. I keep my eyes on the TV because the news is going on and on about the scientific reasons that the fireflies have hung around. According to experts, they've tripled in numbers.

"Extra salt in the air coming in from the coast could be attracting all of these warm-weather-loving bugs!"

"Could be the extra humidity from the coast."

Except, no one seems to *know*.

Dad explains to Mom about the Swiss company that's interested in his newest carburetor invention. "I have to get back to the office sooner than later," Dad says, and dips his garlic bread in his red sauce.

"Mom? What about you?" I ask. "When do you go back to work?" I take a bite of ziti. "Have any fun events coming up?"

Dad lowers his fork and Mom sips on her water.

"What?" I say. "What did I say?"

I check the wall for Mom's event calendar. It's not there. I check for her usual color-coded folders and files filled with seating charts and catering orders. Mom gets up without a word and clears her half-eaten baked lasagna into the trash.

"Your mom left the company," Dad says carefully.

"I took a leave," Mom says, keeping her back to us.

"Why? When?"

"It just got too hard," Mom says.

"Conflict of—" Dad starts to say and I think he's going to say "conflict of interest" but Mom jumps in.

"Not a conflict," she snaps, and walks to the wine refrigerator next to the sink. She pulls out a bottle of white wine. "It was just—time." Mom started that company when she was twenty-five. It was her entire life. What happened?

The wine bottle pops open, and I hear the familiar glug of it being poured into a glass. A memory sparks in my mind, bright in the dark like one of those fireflies in our yard.

Mom drinking.

Mom sad.

Me, disappearing into the theater, into other characters whose lives made sense.

I stand up quickly, and before I even realize what I'm doing, I'm reaching for the bottle.

Mom seems to snap out of her reverie. "What are you doing? Penny, you shouldn't stand up so quickly like that, you could fall." Just as she says it, I stumble back into my chair. The memory that was starting to come back fades away.

"I—I forgot," I mumble.

Mom puts down her glass. "You've had a long day. Maybe we should help you up to bed."

"I want to do it myself," I say.

I stand up again, slowly this time. Dad watches me from the bottom of the stairs. Mom follows close behind in case I fall backward. The cushy carpeting running up the stairs makes it hard for me to sense the landing with my numb foot. I press hard so I can feel that my foot is on the step and move to the next stair using the strength of my left leg. Mom and Dad are silent and I guess it's hard for them to see me dragging my right leg but I need to do it myself.

When I get to the top, Dad joins us, kisses my head but makes sure not to hug me too tight. I know he doesn't want to cause my hand to spasm.

I feel like a bomb about to go off. My hand can spasm at any second, with no warning.

Dad looks concerned. "Maybe I should cancel my meetings this week," he says. We both know he won't, but it's nice that he's even thinking about it.

"You should go," I tell him, and I mean it. "I'll be fine."

He heads downstairs into the basement where I am sure he will stay in his shop for the rest of the night. Mom lingers at the top of the stairs with me.

I look at her smooth, beautiful face, and search for evidence of a year's time passed. Can one year show in a person's face?

"What?" she says with her hand on the doorknob of her bedroom.

"I'm sorry about your job, I didn't remember," I say.

"Don't apologize," Mom says. "I just needed to take a break, for a while."

Mom embraces me and the pressure of her palms against my body, even against my shirt, burns against the figures. She pulls away and I clench my back teeth to mask the pain. Somehow I manage a smile.

"You sure you don't want me to set up your room?" she asks from the doorway.

"I just want to be alone awhile."

"You always have to do it your way," she says with a little shake of her head. "Fine. Get a good night's rest. We have the nurse coming tomorrow, to do PT."

When I go upstairs and step inside the bedroom, it feels like I should recognize it, but I don't. The playbills are gone from the wall near my bed. The ticket stubs, newspaper clippings, and photos of May, Wes, Panda, Karen, and me—gone from the bulletin board above my desk. I limp across the floor and lean my hand on the back of the blue paisley love seat next to the bed.

On the big bulletin board are concert stubs, movie tickets, and *dozens* of photos. I nearly fall forward as I recognize not only the girls in the photos but the voice at the hospital. Kylie Castelli. *Kylie* is my best friend. Mom said it at the hospital, but it's just now sinking in. I remove one of the pushpins holding a photo in place and lift it closer to me. I run my finger down the glossy image: me, Tank Anderson, Kylie Castelli, Lila Suffolk, and Eve Dennings sit on the sea wall in Narragansett, sunglasses on, smiling. These are my *friends*. I can't help but zero in on Kylie's cheek pressed against mine. I grab the next photo and the next . . . Kylie and me in matching bikinis, Kylie and me in matching leather bomber jackets and red lipstick. In another, I am on Tank Anderson's back, red-and-orange leaves litter the ground, and he's in his varsity jacket. God, I look glassy-eyed—like I could be buzzed. *I look like Mom,* a small voice says.

I need my computer. I shuffle some of the papers aside. I recognize English essays and there are a lot of various papers and folders. I check the desk some more, the night table, and anywhere that may have a flat surface where I might leave a laptop.

"Mom!" I call from my bedroom doorway. "Where's my . . ." I am about to say laptop, but I don't know if that's what I have anymore. "Computer," I finish.

"You're not supposed to use it yet," Mom calls. "Remember, no screen time until your eyes recover. You can have it back when Dr. Abrams says it's okay."

I sigh and close my door, then lean against it. My eyes are tired and suddenly I don't have the energy to look at a computer screen anyway, much less argue about it. I know what I'll do. I wasn't ready to open the cards before, but I am now.

I sit down on my bed and pull the unopened cards out of my hospital duffel bag, spreading them in my lap. Each one is an unopened bomb that can explode another truth about who I've been over the last year and a half. I know that—but I need to know. I look around the room at the photos of Kylie, Lila, and Eve.

A card on the top says my name in blue scrawl on a salmon-colored envelope.

I don't know that handwriting—it could be anyone. To open a card, I have to position my hand into a pinching motion, which *could* set off a spasm. But I do it anyway. When I open it, it reads,

Feel better, Penny. We miss your wonderful performances—Ms. Taft

I grab a piece of lined paper from a notebook on the night table. Thankfully, when I flip through quickly, it's blank. I write down a question.

1. Why did I quit theater?

I pause, and add another.

2. How am I friends with Kylie Castelli?

I have about a million more, but I want to finish opening the cards. I tackle the next one, in a pale yellow envelope.

Get better soon, Penny Pen! So glad you are okay—Lila

And then a blue one, after that:

Penny! You are amazing—feel better ASAP!—Eve

Lila Suffolk. Eve Dennings. What the hell *happened* in a year?

I open the last card and on the front is a weird symbol that I don't recognize right away: a white circle against a red background with a lightning bolt through the middle. It looks like the card is handmade. Inside is a message in a messy scrawl I recognize right away even though there was no writing on the front of the card.

Do you think you'll have superpowers like THE FLASH? Get better soon, Berne.—Panda

He's the only one of my old friends to send me a card.

I close my eyes, searching for something, *anything*. I want the memories to come back in a rush like they always do in the movies.

I reread the cards.

My eyes tear up again, blurring the Easter egg–colored assortment of cards in my lap. My nostrils flare, which I hate because I know I'm really on the edge of crying and I'm tired of feeling sorry for myself.

I am going to be strong—Clytemnestra in *Iphigenia* strong. No, I'll be Beatrice from *Much Ado* strong.

I am going to put on the new costume of my life and be grateful I'm alive.

The next day, I blink away the morning light, reach up my arms in a big stretch, and a surprising twinge of pain makes me pull my arms close to my ribs. I sit up quickly to find the source of the ache.

It takes a heartbeat of a moment for me to remember.

Vines and figures curl and tattoo my whole body up to my collarbone.

I look to the massive horizontal windows across the room and push up as fast as I can in my sore state. Something *else* is missing. There should be a mobile made of geodes in the center window. May made it for me in 8th grade. It's hung in the window and glinted in the sunrise every morning since. I limp across the room and draw my fingers to the cool glass.

It's gone. And so is the past year.

Where did I put my theater playbills? I scan the room and check under my bed, pushing aside a black globe and some winter sweaters. I look through my room once more, eventually stopping at my old porcelain dolls. They sit on top of my wooden trunk, not on top of the bureau like they used to. I walk toward the trunk, and lower myself to the floor.

I move the dolls delicately aside so they rest next to one another on the floor. I can't help being gentle with my dolls, no matter how cheesy it is. The top of the trunk creaks open when I flip the latch. Inside the cavernous space are the photo albums, playbills, old scripts, and even parts of costumes from almost every play I've ever done. I sit back on my heels and the figures on my body burn from the pressure. *All* the photos of May and me are in here, hidden in the darkness of this trunk.

I pull out a scrapbook from eighth grade and flip through the pages.

Take a front-row seat! Ocean State Theater Company's star Penny Berne shines as Dorothy.

This garden is flourishing!! Penny Berne as Mary Lennox is riveting!

I stop on a black-and-white newspaper photo of me in sixth grade when I was in *A Christmas Carol.*

I stay on the floor for a long time with the tattered ghosts of my old life.

Photos of May and me sit on the floor near my fingertips. I still know her phone number by heart. It's the password for all of my accounts. My brain *knows* that number. I grab my new cell and turn it on for the first time. It updates with all my old contacts.

I hope to see May's name pop up in my texts. She and I used to exchange hundreds a day. Maybe she didn't send a card because she's been texting me. That makes *so* much sense. A dozen or so text message chimes come in quick succession right away, starting from the first few days I was in the hospital. My heart leaps.

LILA: Wish we could have seen you

KYLIE: Omg. I can't believe the last thing we did was fight.

KYLIE: WHAT IF YOU DIED?

TANK: PENNY! Call me when u get out!

LILA: Dropped your homework at your house!

KYLIE: Penny, I miss you. I called the hospital!

EVE: Lunch is disgusting today. Do they even know what they are serving us?
EVE: Need my running buddy to burn off what I THINK are mashed potatoes!
PANDA: Holy shit, Berne. Your name is a pun!!
KYLIE: I'm sorry, Pen. For everything I said.

With the exception of Panda, I don't know any of these people.

I let the phone rest in my lap and press my fingers against my temples.

The skin on my right leg burns where the first branch of Lichtenberg figures splits and etches out onto my thigh.

Above me in the long, horizontal window, lightning bugs bob in and out of the morning air. No—I'm never calling them that again. Fireflies. That's their name from now on.

If I just keep my eyes closed and concentrate on my breathing, my arms won't ache. My hand won't contract and seize and these branches won't crawl up and over my body.

Maybe if I close my eyes for long enough, none of this will have happened at all.

Once the texts stop coming in and it's silent, I call May. It rings three times. I clench my jaw—too late now. Caller ID will definitely show who is calling.

May picks up.

I open my mouth to say something, but hello and sorry want to come out at the same time so I just croak.

"Penny?" She sounds surprised.

I swallow hard and just launch into it. "May, I'm freaking

out. I don't know what's going on. I lost a lot of memories in the lightning strike. My mom told me we're not friends anymore. I don't remember."

It seems to make sense that she be the first one I tell about my memory loss.

"Your *mom* told you?" She doesn't follow what I am saying. Shivers run over me because I'm sitting in the midst of the scrapbook of our lives and I don't know what to say to my best friend.

"A lot of things happened," she says, and the tone of her voice, while soft, is guarded.

I want to say I'm sorry, but I don't know how to say I am sorry when I don't know what happened between us. I just miss her and the way she makes everything lighter, *funnier* even when I can't see the humor.

"I know I must have done something really stupid. Like quit theater and let you all down," I start to say, but May cuts me off.

"You think that's what happened? You think because you quit theater that we all decided to stop being friends?" When she says it like that, I feel stupid for assuming so.

"I don't know," I go on. "I guess you guys had to pick up the slack or something. I just—" I am about to say, "miss you" when May says, "Look, Penny. I don't want to talk about this when your memory is so messed up. It's not right."

"No, I have to know. I need to know why I have twenty get-well cards and none are from you, Wes, Panda, or Karen. Or why none of my friends came to see me in the hospital."

She takes a deep breath. "Fine. You decided Kylie was a better friend to have. So you ditched Panda, Karen, Wes"—she pauses before she says—"and me. You wanted to party instead of be onstage."

"I wanted to *party*? That sounds made up."

"It felt like that to me for a long time too."

A tear rolls down my cheek and I was so deep in her words I didn't notice I was going to cry. I wipe my nose with the back of my hand, not caring that it's gross and my skin is sticky. "But I don't remember," I whisper. "I don't remember why"—I swallow hard—"we aren't friends."

May stumbles over her words and I hear things like, "secrets," "popular," followed by "you got kinda mean, people didn't want to walk by you in the halls or sit near your crew at lunch."

I don't want to hear anymore.

"You were an ice queen all of a sudden—"

She's midsentence when I hang up.

I lower my cell, placing it back on the carpet next to me. I hold down hard to turn it off so I don't know if she calls me back.

I gently place the newspaper clippings and photo albums back into the trunk in the order I took them out, making sure to close the lid, sealing all the photos, the scrapbooks, and the memories back inside. I rest a shaking hand on top of the trunk. An ice queen?

"Penny!" Dad's voice. "Kylie's here."

My stomach tightens when I hear Kylie say, "Thanks, Mr. B." It's so weird to hear her voice in my house. Now that I've heard it again, it's definitely the same voice from the hospital corridor. God, I don't want her to see the doll collection but my hand isn't strong enough to get them all in and tucked away fast enough. I stand up from the floor and head back to sit at the edge of my bed.

I smell Kylie's perfume first. The rose essential oil that I've coveted since freshman year is made bitter by the overwhelming taste of metal still lingering in my mouth. There's a quick smack of Kylie's flip-flops on the hardwood landing and they stop at my doorway. I haven't covered my arms—it will be the first time anyone other than my parents and the people in the hospital have seen the strange burns on my body. I push up on the bed, scurrying to pull on the cardigan resting on my night table, but it's inside out and I'm not fast enough to slip it over me.

Kylie steps into the room and before "hello" can escape her mouth, her tight puckered lips ease and part. There they are—the figures, twisting across my skin, and shiny from the oodles of burn cream I put on last night. I can't hide my embarrassment.

But Kylie grins.

"Wow!" she says about the figures. "Pen, you are badass."

"Thanks," I say, not sure if that's the right response. I cross the floor to my desk and place the weight in my heel so I am grounded as I walk. It doesn't matter; my right foot drags a little anyway until I lean my hand on the back of the chair for support.

"You're limping," Kylie says. She tries to keep it cool, but it's easy to see concern in her eyes.

"Thanks for trying to come see me at the hospital. I heard your voice, I think, in the hallway."

"Ugh, I was so mad. They wouldn't let me in the ICU."

"I remember," I say. "I remember that."

"I was like, my best friend's in there!"

Kylie plops down on my bed and leans back on her hands. She is in a black tank top and cut-off shorts. She has on what used to be white Converse sneakers but she's drawn crazy designs all over them. My name is in block letters on the sides of the right shoe.

"So what are they?" she asks with a little lift of her voice, and nods to the branches. She is trying to be more casual now that she's gotten over the shock of the figures, which I appreciate.

"Lichtenberg figures. They're like bruises from where the lightning hit. They'll fade eventually." I wonder how many times I am going to have to say this when I get to school. Maybe not so many now that I'm telling Kylie. Her body language makes it obvious that she's been here, at my house, in my room, before. I try to recall it, but I can't. Nothing comes up.

Kylie takes a deep breath. "Look, I'm sorry about what I said at Tank's party. It's exhausting when you don't tell me what's going on. It's like you keep all these secrets. . . ." She is talking so fast I have no idea what to say first or how to respond. She takes a big breath. "And I had to try to put it together on my own."

Put *what* together?

"I watched you act all shady. Your mom would be drinking and you would act like it was no big deal. And it started me thinking about how *I* was acting. And I don't want to be like that, you know? Closed off?"

I'm not closed off, I think, and tuck some hair behind my ears. The spot where the IV was is still tender. Kylie thinks we're friends. She knows about Mom's drinking. She doesn't know about my memory yet. I have to tell her something.

"So when you were being all dodgy, I just snapped." She exhales really sharply. "Sorry," she says. "I've been wanting to get that out forever."

"I'm sorry too," I finally say. "For whatever I did. But . . ." She looks up at me, waiting for me to finish. "I don't actually *know* what I did."

"What do you mean?" She grins. "Too drunk to remember the party? Maybe I was wrong about one and done?"

"No," I say, and I want to pace but my numb foot makes it hard to talk and walk at the same time. "Not just the party."

"Oh, I bet you can't remember the night of the strike. They say that can happen after traumatic accidents, right?" Kylie asks.

Kylie's eyes follow all of my movements and I don't want to lie to her.

"It's a lot more complicated than that," I say.

"What do you mean?"

I can't explain it but I feel like I owe her the truth. "I can't remember anything from the last year. Since last May, actually."

Her grin fades. "What are you talking about?"

"The lightning . . . it affected my memory."

She frowns and it makes her features sharp. Thick mascara is the only makeup she seems to be wearing. She blinks hard and her mouth makes a tiny O shape as she understands what I am saying.

"May of last year?" she repeats. "Like before eleventh grade?" Her voice rises an octave.

I taste metal more than ever. I want lemonade or a lollipop.

She crosses her arms over her chest. "You don't remember Tank's party?"

I shake my head. She doesn't want to believe it.

"The Howl shows at the Joint?"

Again, no.

"My house? Pool parties? Riding around on Tank's tractor? Smoking weed in Patelli's basement?"

No. No. No. No. No.

"Fuck!" she cries. "Do you remember being friends with me?"

I whisper it this time. "No."

She flinches at my response and stands up. My shame sits on my shoulders.

"I'm sorry," I say, because I am. I'm so sorry.

Perfect, popular Kylie Castelli's eyes tear up and she looks down at the bedspread.

"You don't remember being friends." She has her hand over her mouth. It's only then that I see she's wearing a ring, a thin silver band with a small blue stone. It's identical to the one I'm wearing. They gave it to me at the hospital but I hadn't thought much of it. I assumed it was a gift from Mom and Dad.

If I try really hard, maybe something will come, some shred of memory from the past year. I will it from the darkness. I struggle for any clue, but my mind is pitch-black and I can't find my way to the light.

My legs aren't strong enough, so I have to sit down. I grip the bedpost with my left hand. I have to press my heels into the floor to steady myself. If I grip too tight I might set off a spasm.

"I don't know what happened. Or why I stopped hanging

out with my friends." I quickly rebound when she flinches. "My other friends. You know, May Harper, Panda Thomas, Wes Peterson . . ."

Kylie's frown sets even deeper. "You said you didn't want to be in theater anymore. That you wanted something different," she explains.

I take a step closer to Kylie.

"When? When did I say that?"

She drops her eyes and searches the floor.

"All the time."

"*All* the time?" I repeat. "I don't talk to Wes? Or May? Or anyone from the theater?"

"No. Not really."

"Why? There has to be some reason!"

She slaps her hands to her thighs. "God, Penny. *I'm* standing right here."

"I'm sorry. I'm so sorry. You're right."

After a moment she explains, "There's not much to tell. My car broke down. You picked me up. I took you to Alex James's party. That was the night we became friends—we've been friends ever since."

"Alex James? The guy who always wears bright-colored Polos?"

"He asked you out right before Tank's party. We were dying over it. Penny? Remember?" I don't know what she reads from my expression but her eyes widen. "God, you *really* don't remember, do you?"

"I wish I did. I remember you from school and stuff. It's

just . . . Kylie, I don't *know* you."

Kylie breaks into a sob and turns, running for the door. "I have to go," she cries.

"Kylie, wait!" I call, and move too quickly. The screaming, needling pain blasts from the center of my right palm. The seizing comes in waves. The pain cuts off my words. The muscles in my palm clench so tight that my fingers are drawn together, straight and awkward. I have to bend over to tolerate the pain.

I yell out and fall to my knees in the middle of the room. My back shudders and my fingers close, pinching together tighter and tighter, until the fingertips touch. The spasms run from my neck to my tailbone.

I cry out and heavy footsteps run up the stairs. Not Mom's, but Dad's.

"It's okay," he says, and wraps his hands around me to steady the pain. "It's okay, Penny. Just breathe."

But I can't.

NINE

THAT MONDAY MORNING BEFORE SCHOOL STARTS, I finally get access to my computer for a carefully timed twenty minutes.

My online accounts show a world that has existed, up until now apparently, only in my wildest imagination.

In many of the photos, Kylie and I drink from the same bottle of vodka at parties, wear matching leather jackets at concerts, and have coordinating face paint at football games. In each photo Lila and Eve are in the background, but *we* are in the foreground of the picture, arms draped around each other. We are the stars. We're clearly best friends.

It's weird but—I'm jealous of this photograph version of me.

It's been ten days since I was struck in Tank's pool. Ten days that I have been covered with these markings, and that my memory has been blank. On the computer, I scroll back through all the days I was in the hospital, through the well wishes and various notes. I stop when I get to the feed from the night of the strike.

There's a photo of Kylie and me wearing dark crimson lipstick. We make kissy faces in the rearview mirror of a car. That's right! I can drive! I missed my sixteenth birthday. I scroll back up to the top of the page and do a double take at some of the posts right before the lightning strike. I actually scoot closer to the monitor.

Congrats on homecoming nom!

You were nominated, Penny!

I was nominated for homecoming queen? I wait to be excited. I should want to jump up and down in my seat.

But I'm not. I fixate on the names of the people writing me messages. None of them are people I know. Acquaintances, sure, but none of them are my friends.

I scroll back as many months as I can, but it's a flutter of posts that all look similar. Kylie and I are out at live music shows or riding around in my car or hers.

I keep going and the first post is from late May, 2015. Right after I quit *Much Ado About Nothing.*

"Penny!" Dad calls. "Let's go! We don't want to be late for your meeting!"

I've had online accounts since seventh grade—the year Mom let me get my own laptop. But there's *no* evidence of the two years before this. I must have deleted my original accounts and started new ones. A memory, like a firefly, darts around in my head. If I could only catch it, I might be able to figure out how any of this happened. But that firefly darts deeper into the black of my mind and pulses like a faraway star. If only I could get to it.

I close the laptop cover; I don't want to look anymore.

After a minute or two, I'm almost done with my morning rituals of burn cream and medication. Last but not least, the superfun process of getting dressed. I stand before the clothes in my closet, but I don't recognize a single item on a hanger. I tug at a pair of jeans and pull them closer to me. *La Brea?* Kylie is always wearing them. These are the most ridiculously expensive designer jeans and I have *two pairs* in my closet. I sit on the bed and pull the jeans on. The fabric suctions to my leg. With a tug upward using my left hand, the tight denim sears along the vines on my skin.

"Holy hell!" I cry out, and kick them off. They coil on the ground near my feet. I rub some silver sulfadiazine cream to help with the stinging burns.

I grab a pair of leggings and slip them on instead. The fabric is soft against my skin. Even though they stop at the ankle, I use some stage makeup I find in the trunk to cover the last branches that coil onto the top of my foot. After slipping on a tank top and a long-sleeved cardigan, even though it's seventy-five degrees out, I tap a little concealer along my collarbone as well. I limp to the bedroom door.

Last night, after another round of the burn cream for my

figures, Mom gave me a fresh bag of fruit-flavored sucking candies. I still taste metal no matter how much sweet gum or lemonade I have. I eat a cherry one anyway and throw the rest in my school bag.

I trudge down the stairs slowly. Even with the makeup covering my skin, I'm still self-conscious about my limp.

The streets are nearly empty as we drive up toward school. It's well before any students will be there because I get to kick off my first day back with an early-morning meeting with the headmaster, my teachers, and the school counselor.

"I guess they're going to want to talk to me about everything," I say.

Dad sighs. "Look, Pen. Your mom and I wanted you to find out from us first, and well, your mom slept in today, but I—"

"What?" I say, and turn to him. I forgot to move slowly; the figures ache and I suck in a sharp breath. "I'm okay," I say quickly. "What's going on?" Dad pulls onto the path that leads up to the double doors of the school. "You said the meeting was to get me up to speed and get back on track."

"Are you sure you don't want me to come?" Dad says. We're idling outside school. "You can take more time off. We can homeschool."

"*What's* going on, Dad?"

He pushes his glasses up the bridge of his nose.

"They have to put you on a probationary period as a senior. We don't know how much information you've retained and what you've lost since the strike. Or if it will affect how you learn new things."

My heart sinks. "They're keeping me back?"

All I can see in my head are Wes, May, Panda, and Karen, walking across the stage at graduation without me. I grip the seat cushion but the middle of my right hand zings and I have to relax. Except, they're not my friends anymore. I try to picture myself walking across the stage with Kylie, Lila, and Eve, but it doesn't feel the same.

"No. They're not holding you back—not yet, anyway. But they've taken you out of AP for now."

"But I've always been on the honors track. I worked so hard—"

"I know, I know. But Pen, eleventh grade was really hard academically and we don't know yet what you've kept and what you might have lost. We just have to wait and see."

"I just want my life back," I say.

"I know. Just go in and talk to them, and you can call me after to let me know what happens." He pauses. "But I really think I should come with you."

"I have to do this myself," I say, and look up at the double doors. "I have to."

Dad nods and kisses me on the forehead. He pulls away to rummage in the backseat for something.

I double-check that I have the stage makeup concealer in my bag so I can cover any stray ferns throughout the day. I don't want the headmaster, or anyone for that matter, to see them and think I need to be kept back. I am about to open the car door when Dad says, "Wait. I got you something." He pulls out a small brown paper bag. I pull out a leather-bound journal with my initials engraved in tiny gold letters on the front: PLB.

"I *love* it," I say.

"Dr. Abrams said you should do your best to note any inconsistencies with your memory. I thought you could use a journal to keep track of it all." He smiles. "And I thought it was cool."

"It *is* cool," I say. "Thanks." I kiss him quickly on the cheek and let him go back home to write his typical nine thousand emails to people about his new inventions.

"You can call or text me after the meeting?" he says through the window, once I'm already out of the car.

"Text you?" I say. "Do you do that now?"

"I try but I'm not that hip," he says. "Lots of typos."

"Get with the times, Dad," I say, and note the irony of my situation with a cringe.

"Hey! She's already back to punning!"

I laugh, and limp my way up toward school.

"Well, I think it's important that we be realistic here." The headmaster's voice is as annoying as ever. Six thirty and I'm sitting here in between Headmaster Lewis, School Counselor Ms. Winters, and Ms. Reley, who's been assigned as my faculty advisor while I readjust to school. Reley is notorious for being a hard-ass. Yippee.

"Penny was third in her class last year," Reley says.

I *was*?

"She'll catch up quickly."

"I just don't know," Headmaster Lewis says with a shake of his head. "It's a lot of work to make up."

"Know what?" Reley retorts, and I can hear the aggravation

in her voice. "The state said it's our discretion given her academic record. We've already taken her out of accelerated classes."

"Look." Ms. Winters sighs. She seems to be sighing her way through this whole meeting. "I think we should hold off on taking any drastic measures like holding Penny back a year until we see just how permanent her memory loss is. We might be overreacting for nothing."

I nod. I like that idea.

Headmaster Lewis flips through a file folder, which I would love to get my hands on. Over the top, I can see a typed letter with the Memorial Hospital logo.

"Penny's memory loss is very extensive," Headmaster Lewis says. "And eleventh grade is an important year academically. I fear without the memory of last year, she won't be adequately prepared for college next year."

"She may not remember the events of last year but it doesn't mean that her development and skill set are compromised," Ms. Winters explains, and I hope that it's true.

"What do you want to do, Penny?" Ms. Reley asks.

I can hear the chatter from the hallway as it begins to fill up with people.

"It's strange. I feel like I should be in eleventh grade and taking my SATs. The timing feels off. But I want to be with my friends. I want to be with—" I am about to say their names: Wes, May, Panda, and Karen. "I need to get back to the way things were. Apply to college," I say quietly.

The headmaster looks thoughtful. "If we keep you where you are, we'll need to establish some ground rules to help you succeed academically." He ticks things off on his fingers. "Someone will have to get Penny up to speed on her standardized testing scores and work with her on her college applications."

That's right. I took the SATs already.

"We will also need to provide her with a note-taking buddy and a peer tutor."

An idea rushes into my head. I know the *perfect* tutor.

"May I suggest someone?" I ask.

"I don't see why not," Headmaster Lewis says. "It will need to be someone you work well with, after all."

"May Harper would be great."

They all share a glance, one that says, *bad idea*. After a pause, Ms. Winters says, "We'll check with May today. If she agrees, we'll get you guys working straightaway."

The meeting is adjourned and I limp out of the room. I hesitate before stepping out of the administrative offices and into the hallway. I don't know who I will sit with at lunch or who will make room for me. I haven't heard from Kylie since she ran out of my bedroom. I sit down in a chair near the doorway. In my new notebook, I write down the two questions from last night and scribble a third question below the other two:

1. Why did I quit theater?
2. How am I friends with Kylie Castelli?

The third is probably the most important . . .

3. How do I apologize and get my friends back?

TEN

WHEN I WALK INTO THE HALLWAY THE ENDLESS streams of bodies just getting out of homeroom are a welcome camouflage. Phones ding and beep, girls near me squeal about their dresses for homecoming, and my thoughts are drowned in the slam of locker doors. I walk slowly so as not to draw any attention to the limp, and make sure to pull down on the sleeves of my cardigan to cover any of the ferns that could accidentally show.

Concentrate on the center of your foot, press down, and repeat. It's useless. I might as well not have any toes. I smooth any fly-aways on the top of my head and even though I curled my hair this morning the humidity makes it fall flat. I don't *think* I look like I was almost fried twelve days ago.

I'm heading toward my locker when someone cries my name.

"Penny! You're back!" Eve runs toward me. She's got long blond hair now, not the chin-length bob I remember.

"Do you know me?" a different girl says, and runs at me too. She has black hair with dyed green tips. I don't know her. "Kylie told me you don't remember anyone!"

"How about me?" asks a girl whose features seem familiar but I can't place her either.

"I . . ." I start to say, but more and more people circle around me.

You look amazing!

What happened?

Do you remember the lightning?

Penny *Penny!*

Penny!

Penny!

Penny

Penny!

Penny

I bring my hand to my head and cover my eyes. I keep my eyes clenched shut. My stomach lurches. People touch my forearms and shake my hand and I feel pressure on my skin, even under the long sleeves of my cardigan. It burns.

I try to walk but Eve gives me a side hug and my knees nearly buckle at the wash of heat that rolls over my ribs when she squeezes me. I glance around, searching for a familiar face, but people either are nearly on top of me, or they pass too quickly for me to pick anyone out. Metal-flavored saliva rushes into my mouth.

"Okay, okay! Break it up. Coming through." Panda's voice booms through the air. He parts the crowd. "Come on," he says, and pushes both his arms out to make room for me. I rush through.

"Thanks," I say breathlessly.

Eve calls after me, "I'll see you at lunch!"

I want to stay and talk to Panda, but my skin is on fire and if I don't get this cardigan off me, right now, I am going to lose it. Another flush of heat rolls over me and I limp as fast as I can down the hall, turn away from all the well-wishers and into the quiet of the hallway where the art studios are. There are no art classes during this time block, and most days it's deserted. Alone, I can finally breathe.

I lean my head back against the cement wall. I slip the cardigan off my shoulders so I'm just wearing a black tank top, exposing my chest, neck, and arms. The cool air on my skin nearly makes my knees buckle from relief.

"I can do this," I whisper. I just have to get through a few classes. I can keep up with the work. I know I can. "I can do this," I say again.

Someone clears his throat. Wes steps out from an art room at the end of the hall.

I jump up, pulling my cardigan to my chest.

"I just needed a second," I say, trying to explain why I'm ripping off my clothes in the middle of a hallway.

He walks to me; he is so much taller than I remember. In my head he's still kind of lanky, standing on the stage with a script in his hand. But he's changed in a year. This version of Wes is muscular. Older. He stops across from me and digs his hands deep in his pockets.

"How are you?" he says.

"Okay, Gumby. You?"

A tiny smile tugs at his mouth as he meets my eyes. His gaze pauses on the figures on my arms and stomach. His eyes trace along my shoulder and stop, focusing on my collarbone.

"They're called Lichtenberg figures," I say quietly. I'm not sure if he cares.

He clears his throat, breaking his gaze away from my skin. I lean forward, drawn by the scruff of facial hair on his chin. I want to touch him. For a second, we look into each other's eyes. There's hurt in his expression.

"How are—" I start.

He squeezes his eyes closed like pain has rushed through him and he backs away quickly. I immediately slip the cardigan over my shoulders with a sore lift of my arms.

"I have to go," he says, and hurries down the hall, around the corner, and away.

"I'm sorry," I whisper, but it's too late, he's gone, and the heat between us crackles outward into the air, away from me.

Dr. Abrams has explicitly instructed me not to drive for *two weeks*, which is fine by me because I only had a permit the last I remember. So, after school, Bettie drops me off at home before heading home herself. There's a black Honda in the driveway that I don't recognize.

Just as I open the door to step into the kitchen, I hear Dad talking to a man whose voice I can't identify. "Mr. Berne, I'm sorry to bother you, but I'm Troy Fellizi from Channel Six News." The man's voice comes from the living room.

"I was hoping to speak to your daughter when she comes home from school. I'd love to interview her for our morning news program. It's a real survivor story," he explains.

I step out to the screened-in porch attached to our kitchen so I can listen better. I hold my backpack close to my body so nothing inside will jingle or clank.

"She's still recovering, and I'm not sure she's ready for visitors just yet. Can you show me some of your credentials?" Dad says.

There's the sound of latches like the journalist is opening a briefcase.

"I don't think Penny will want to be on TV." Mom's voice. "Besides, we would rather not draw attention to Penny's aesthetic reactions to the strike." Of course Mom would be concerned about how it *looks.*

"Aesthetic?" the journalist asks.

"She has some markings on her skin," Mom explains.

Great. So now the public will know that I've got ferns all over me. I crack open the door and tiptoe into the empty kitchen.

"I'd also love a chance to catch up with you, Mrs. Berne. What are your present plans? Will you be returning to the event planning industry?"

God, this guy is good.

"Can I offer you some water? Coffee?" Mom says.

"Water would be great," the reporter says, and Mom's soft footsteps pad from the living room and she stops, freezing when she sees me standing just outside the kitchen door with my bag held to my chest. She must be able to tell from the expression on my face that I heard what happened in the living room.

"Do you want him to interview you?" she mouths.

I shrug. It might not be bad to tell people what happened.

"I don't want him to take pictures of my skin," I say.

She nods. "We won't let him."

"Okay," I say. "I guess that would be all right." She leads me into the living room. I note as we walk in that there are no wine bottles in the wine chiller or any glassware in the bottom of the sink. I know she pulled a bottle out the night we got back from the hospital, but I don't think she ever opened it.

Maybe things really have changed?

The next morning before school, I root through the bag I had with me in the hospital. At the bottom is my hospital bracelet. I tape it to the second lined page in the journal that Dad gave me. As I'm putting the journal in my school bag, I notice a pile of books on the floor next to my desk. Some of the items in the pile are binders from last year's classes. On the very top is my day planner. Nice! If anything, there might be some answers in there about what happened between my friends and me.

"Penny!" Bettie calls, and I slip the day planner in my school bag too.

I double-check to make sure my long-sleeved shirt covers my

figures, and only when I am adjusting it does someone knock on my door.

I expect it to be Dad but Bettie walks in.

"Your friend is here to drive you to school."

I immediately think of Wes, but that's not possible.

"My friend?" I ask.

I peek outside.

"You've got to be kidding me," I say at the sight of a lime green Lexus with Panda in the driver's seat. I limp downstairs and note on the way that Mom is still sleeping. Dad is already in his basement shop, working.

When I get outside to Panda's car, I run my hand down the custom paint job. No one would *sell* a car in this color, let alone *buy* one.

"*When* did you get this monstrosity?" I say through the open window.

"Well, Miss Memory Challenged," Panda says, and with a click the doors unlock. "I got it last year with the money I got for a voice-over commercial."

"You could have sprung for a more subtle paint job."

He laughs. "Get in."

My thighs shake as I bend and slip into the car. The car is a complete shit show inside. Although it doesn't surprise me, there are at least ten different types of potato chip bags on the floor. I pull down on the arms of my shirt.

He hands over a coffee. "Just the way you like it."

I sip on it and inhale the roasted but bitter coffee.

"Wow, is it bad or something?"

"What?" I say. "No, it's really good." I force another sip.

"You're full-on grimacing, Berne. If I wasn't driving, I'd take it from you."

We head out of my neighborhood and past the marina. In another mile we'll be at school.

I grip the warm cup between my hands.

"So . . ." I say casually. "How long have I been drinking black coffee? You know, like this?"

"Last year," he says, and I nod and force another sip. The last I remembered, I usually drank London Fogs. Earl Grey tea, vanilla syrup, and steamed milk.

After a few twists and turns of the road, Panda pulls into the EG Private parking lot. When he puts the car in park he looks over at me. Concern on Panda's face makes his round features seem smaller.

I unclick my seat belt and place the coffee in the cup holder so I can open the door with my left hand. Panda scoots out and around to the passenger side. By the time he gets to my door I'm nearly out of the car. I don't usually see Panda serious—hardly ever. He's barely speaking above a whisper when he says, "Berne. How are you?"

"I'm here. I just want to be normal, whatever that means. I don't want people making special accommodations for me or anything."

"Well, that's something." His eyebrows rise.

"What?"

"You. With the volunteering information."

I don't understand this at all. "What do you mean?"

"You're not big on giving up information about yourself. You know, when *emotions* are involved."

"So I hear," I say. Panda opens the car door for me fully and I'm grateful to get out too. Panda swings his bag so it's tighter on his back and begins the walk to school. He's a couple of paces up when he glances back and sees I haven't moved from the car. He's wearing a black T-shirt with an enormous image of a person in cat makeup from the Broadway show *Cats*.

"Why did you come get me today?" I ask and start walking.

Panda doesn't seem to want to answer me right away. I stop, touching his arm lightly. "Come on, Panda. My other friends won't talk to me, but you do."

He breathes heavily through his nose.

"Okay, but I'm not going into detail. It's too hard. *For me.*"

"Okay," I say gently, and sort of wish I hadn't asked.

"Because you stood up to my dad once last year."

"I did?"

"Yeah, when he found out I was staying back."

"You stayed *back*!?"

"Gee, thanks for your sensitivity."

I squeeze his arm and walk again. It feels better to have uncomfortable conversations when I'm moving.

"I'm sorry," I say.

"Ever wonder why I was the one people went to for drugs?" He reads the confusion on my face because he adds quickly, "No. No, you don't. Look, Berne, I was in rehab from July through August this summer. Did a bunch of drugs. Sold 'em too, when I was feeling generous. It wasn't pretty."

"Oh, Panda, I'm so sorry."

We walk in silence for a moment. I hike my book bag over my shoulder.

I look around for Richard or for May's white Mini Cooper. Most everyone has gone inside for homeroom and Panda and I are two of the few people left in the parking lot. I see the Mini a few rows down and it occurs to me that maybe Panda and I are alone because Richard didn't want to ride with us. It's almost like Panda reads my mind as he hesitates before the double doors.

"They'll come around eventually. You're a good egg, Berne," he says as the bell rings, signaling the end of homeroom.

"I don't . . ." I say, and he drops his hand from the door handle. "I don't know why I acted the way I did. But I don't want to become her ever again. Just remind me. Keep me in check, okay?"

"You know I will," he says, and it's enough to break my heart. "Now can we go to school? I'm already on Headmaster Lewis's shit list."

ELEVEN

AT THIRD PERIOD, I'M IN THE HALLWAY OUTSIDE the library entrance, waiting for May. I don't want to be sitting in there alone so I'm practicing my balance and leaning against the wall. I kept expecting to see May in some of my classes, but I guess she's in AP. Even with Panda's promise, I know you can't *make* anyone do something they don't want to do. Mom used to say that to me constantly when I was a kid: "You can't make people love you, Penny." Funny, because I always felt like if I tried hard enough, I could get anyone to like me. Once I met May I didn't have to worry about working so hard to make people like me anymore.

I check my watch just as Kylie turns a corner, flipping through a binder from our school radio station. I clutch my books, not sure what to say. Her eyes stab up at me just as Karen walks in from an adjacent classroom. I pull my long sleeves down to make sure my wrists and arms are still covered. Karen stops short just in front of me, unintentionally cutting Kylie off. Kylie's jaw drops and she hurries past. "Wait!" I say, but she's already gone. But I want to talk to Karen too.

Karen takes a deep breath through her nose, so much so that I can see her chest rise and fall. "How are you?" she asks.

"Still here," I say, laughing awkwardly.

"Good. That's really good." But her tone, while cordial, is empty. I push off from the wall.

"You look great. No more braces," I add.

She softens at this. "Yeah, I got them off last summer. I'm sorry to hear about your memory."

I nod—she nods. We walk into the library, so having something to do with my body helps with the awkwardness. There's more awkward silence, until she says, "I guess I'll see you."

I lower myself into a seat as she leaves. That was nice and uncomfortable. I make a point to make a note about that interaction in my journal. I get my books and papers together, checking the time—May is ten minutes late.

Just as I think she won't come at all, May sweeps into the library with her long black hair flying behind her. "Sorry I'm late," she says, and she's out of breath.

The double doors open again and Kylie and Lila walk through them. I press down harder on the tip of my pen as they walk toward our table.

"Hey," I say to Kylie as she passes by, careful not to miss this opportunity. She glances at May and throws me a half-assed smile. She heads into the stacks without a word. Eve, who basically mauled me yesterday, doesn't even acknowledge me.

May unpacks her bag and when she tucks her hair behind her ear I say, "You got the top of your ear pierced. You always wanted to. It looks cool," I say.

"I got it last January," May says coolly, and slides a manila folder across the table to me.

"What's this?"

"No idea. I was told not to open it. Ms. Reley says you're supposed to check in with her at the end of the day."

I open the manila envelope and an official red sheet falls onto the table. May tries to hide it, but as she gets out her books and notebooks, she glances at the sheet too.

SAT SCORE: 1510.

"What!" I screech, and a few heads look up from around the library. A 1510 is *incredible.* Who knew I could standardize test so well?

May cocks her head. "What happened?"

"Oh. It's just my SAT scores."

"Not good?"

I shrug. I don't want to be too cocky. "It's no big deal."

"Of course. SAT scores. No big deal," May says sarcastically. "Anyway . . ." She immediately launches into the expectations that we have in each class by going over the syllabi for English, history, math, and science. Though when I look at my eleventh grade schedule, I note that I took AP Spanish too. I guess all the free time I would have spent in rehearsals was spent studying instead. There's no way for me to know for sure but it makes sense, though—AP classes *and* a 1510 on my SATs? They don't think I can handle the AP level now.

It takes time, Dr. Abrams says in my head.

May is all business for the next thirty minutes. When she's done reviewing math concepts, I understand how to do some of the problems but will definitely need a special tutor for math. I note that May is filling out a sheet of some kind with the EG Private logo at the top. She says that we will have to meet at the end of the week to see if I can keep up with the pace in history, but I do pretty solid on her mini quiz from this week's class content.

She goes on and on. My journal pokes out of the top of my bag, reminding me what I need to do.

"May."

She stops midsentence.

"I'm sorry."

She closes the folder with all our work and the extra-help handouts from my teachers.

"I know," she says gently.

"All I say to people is I'm sorry."

She nods but something in her expression is sour.

"It's not like I think people should forget. It's just . . ."

She isn't looking at me.

"They told me you asked for me directly," she says.

"So I could talk to you."

"Oh." When she looks up, her eyes, which I remember as always having a hint of a laugh behind them, are hard. "I can't say no to the school counselor. You know that."

I consider what she says. "Yeah, I guess that makes sense. I wouldn't want to say no to Ms. Winters either."

"You *guess* that makes sense? You put me in a crappy position."

I really don't want that to be true. I imagine myself in her shoes and I wouldn't want to be pressured into this situation either. I groan.

"You're right," I say.

She gathers her things, and when she stands up, she leaves a hand on her chair. I don't want her to leave, so I press up on my left hand, hoping that I have the strength to get up without my arm shaking.

"I have no way of knowing what to be sorry about. But I am. Believe me. The last thing I remember was you and me at *Much Ado About Nothing* rehearsal."

"I know that you're sorry. *That* Penny, the one you remember? I do think she would be sorry." She looks me up and down. "But you're freaking out right now and I don't know if you're sorry because you're desperate or sorry because you miss me."

"You know I miss you."

"No," she says, and she isn't even whispering anymore. "I don't. Because you said you were sorry before and it didn't sound like it when you kept huge secrets from your friends or made me learn Beatrice's lines in two days. Or the day you sat down at Kylie's table at lunch and when I came up to you, you didn't make room for me. Or my personal favorite? When you basically kicked me out of a party at Tank's house."

"Stop. It's horrible," I say.

"Yeah. It is. Especially when we watched your mom's story on the news," May says just as the librarian comes out from behind the reference desk. "You refused to let any of us in. You shut down completely."

"My mom's story? What are you talking about?"

"Forget it," she says.

"The news ran stories on my mom?" But May just turns and leaves the library. I almost call out to her, but I don't—I let her walk away.

If the local news ran stories on Mom then it doesn't sound like she "took a leave."

I feel like a stranger in my own life.

I have to believe that getting my life back is possible. Panda's words about what I did for him are the only shining light. I'm *not* the girl in the stories that May just told me. I'm better than that.

I have to be.

I try the outside cafeteria at lunch. There are five or six tables out here that are adjacent to the football fields. I've been out here a zillion times. I used to sit closest to the soda and vending machine near the far wall so Panda could get mini chip bags. I sit down at a free table at the edge of the fields. I check for Panda but he told me he has a weekly lunch meeting with Ms. Winters. The double doors open behind me, and Kylie, Lila, Eve, and some of the other girls step out, but they hesitate when they see me. Lila locks eyes on me first and turns to Kylie, tucking her chin close to Kylie's ear. I guess that's not a good sign. Eve and

Caroline Hester follow behind Kylie, but the sight of their ponytails tightens my stomach. Kylie, the only one without a ponytail, flips her hair over her shoulder, glances at me, and much to my surprise, walks directly over to the table.

Lila sits down beside me, and Eve next to her. Kylie makes a point to sit down across the table from Lila, leaving the space in front of me empty.

"Sorry about today in the hallway. I needed to talk to Karen," I say.

"Got it," she says with a disinterested shrug. I can't read her; she's always been so far away to me—unattainable. The girl who I would have nothing in common with so I just stayed far away. She unpacks a small salad and just when she opens up her dressing, Kylie jumps in her seat, reanimating, with her eyes locked on Lila and Eve.

"Oh my god. I just remembered. I have to see this show on Friday at the Joint."

"You say that like it's unusual," Eve says with a laugh.

"Anyway," Kylie stresses the word, "it's this blues band, but they've got a funk sound. I think the lead guitarist is classically trained so their stuff is really complicated."

Kylie mentions the kind of instruments they use and the specific equipment. She knows so much more about music than I realized.

"What time?" Lila asks.

"Nine, I think," Kylie replies.

Kylie gestures with her hands, excitedly slapping her palms on the table. "Penny, we absolutely have to—"

Not even the outside cafeteria chatter can make up for the silence between us when Kylie stops herself midsentence.

She drops her chin to her chest and throws her hair over her shoulder again. "Habit," she says, and her cheeks are red.

"We used to go see live music shows a lot," Lila explains to me.

"I know."

Kylie's eyes snap up to me and hope prickles in her expression.

"I have lots of pictures. In my room and online."

I focus down at the lunch I brought from home: celery with peanut butter inside like I might be some kind of first grader. It's just easy to pick up and chew without setting off a spasm.

"Penny Berne! Love of my life!" Alex James says, busting out of the double doors of the school. He sits down next to Kylie so he's directly across from me. "Remember that day we shared on the tennis courts?"

"You don't want to, Penny, seriously," Lila says with a laugh and Eve laughs too; she even makes eye contact.

"You dick, you know she doesn't," Kylie snaps at Alex, and for a second I'm grateful that I could like sitting here at this table with them.

But then I have a strange thought. They didn't sit with me because we're friends. It hits me that I've sat down at *Kylie's* table without knowing it. Did I know, on some level, that this used to be our table? But Kylie thought I was purposefully sitting here with her. I don't know which role to play or which costume to wear when the script of my life has been revised without my consent.

There's another bang of the doors when Tank Anderson and a slew of football players head outside and toward the table.

"Hey! Penny Berne! You're back!" Tank says. He sits down. "You coming to my party this Friday?"

A party at Tank's? I'd feel so out of place. Even though I guess they're all my friends, it doesn't feel that way to me.

"I think I'm busy," I say. "Next time, though."

"Don't let me down, Berne!" he says, and claps a hand on my shoulder, and before I know what's happened I'm doubled over in pain. With a sharp tug, my hand freezes—the fingers draw together immediately and I howl. I try to get up but fall to my knees, cradling my elbow to my body.

The pain is a needle stuck in the center of my palm.

Reley is on her knees by my side, seemingly out of nowhere. I register that other people are nearby. Tank keeps apologizing. I press down on my fingers but my left hand isn't strong enough to pry them apart. Tank comes down to his knees on the other side of me. I can't look at him, not with the pain shooting through my hand. The pinching spasm isn't lessening up yet.

"Tank!" Kylie cries. "What the hell did you do?"

"I didn't know," Tank says, and my stomach tugs at the apology in his tone.

"What can I do?" Reley asks me.

"Nothing," I groan, and push at my fingers to relieve the raging stabs of pain in the center of my hand. I hunch over to keep my back to the caff. I exhale a few times as my heartbeat pulses in the center of my palm. My back is tight from clenching so hard.

The muscles ease just enough that I can speak without gritting my teeth. "I get these spasms when I move too quickly," I groan. Eventually, within a few moments . . . my palm releases and my fingers do too. My hairline is wet and when I lift my right arm to wipe my forehead, my bicep shakes and my fingers *finally* loosen fully. Ms. Reley deflates with a big sigh. I sit back on my butt with my hand resting, limp, in my lap.

"What just happened?" Eve whispers.

I push up with my left hand to stand. As I do, May walks outside holding a bagged lunch.

"Someone should walk you to the nurse," Reley says.

May and I lock eyes.

Reley must notice me looking at May because she twists to follow my gaze. "May Harper!" Reley calls to her. "May will take you."

"Okay," I say quietly. "Thanks." After her outburst in the library, I'm not quite as enthusiastic about being alone with my former best friend.

I struggle to stay upright. I make sure to put as much weight as possible on my good leg. Once I get to May, she holds open the door. My eyes burn with tears but I bite them back by clenching my jaw. I can't look back at Kylie when I have so clearly chosen May to help me, who I know would rather not.

"I'm okay," I say once I get inside.

"What happened?"

"A spasm," I say, and I can't walk fast enough, especially with the weakness in my right foot. I use my heel to limp a bit more quickly.

"What was that on her skin?" I hear Eve say as the doors close.

Rattled and vibrating, my abs shake as I keep on down the hall.

May slows at my side, falling a few steps behind. I can't look her in the face either.

"Penny . . ." she says finally, falling behind. "Should I walk you?"

I'm so tired of pity.

"I'm fine," I say, knowing I'm not going to the nurse's office. Nope. I'm going the only place where my life still makes a shred of sense.

TWELVE

THE DOOR TO THE AUDITORIUM CLOSES SLOWLY behind me. I must have looked so stupid hobbling out of the outside cafeteria. What kind of person attempts to run when they have a limp that actually prevents them from moving with any kind of speed? I collapse down in a chair at the end of the last row. I throw my books to the floor so they slam and the sound echoes in the vacant and dark auditorium. There is a ghost light in the center of the stage. Taft does this whenever there is a show about to go up. It's a single light bulb on a stand to prevent anyone from falling in the dark. I pull my planner from last year out of my backpack. I flip it open even though my hand still throbs.

Wow.

Every event and date from May through August is color-coded. Blue for school commitments, green for extracurricular, and red for Kylie. I gave Kylie her own *color*? I flip back to the month of May. In nearly every box, I scheduled my day, and it's all the same: gym, track, and Kylie's house. If it's the summer it's gym, beach, and Kylie's house. The words "beach," "pool," and "party" are written everywhere in my unmistakable red print. When the hell did I become this anal? Nowhere, not even when I flip back to January, does it mention anything about Wes, May, or any play.

What. The. Hell. Happened?

I flip through the green and red sections, which seem to be the most common colors of the whole planner. I look through the pockets of the planner, check the notes, but the only thing I seemed to care about from May until now was going out with Kylie, parties, and occasional mentions of homecoming.

I flip to the last page of notes and stop. My Common App username and password are scribbled, and then beneath it:

1. Bates
2. Skidmore
3. Bowdoin

In small letters at the bottom of the page is: NYU?

These can't be the schools I am applying to, can they? It's not possible. I would have chosen schools with a specialized theater conservatory. Sure, some of them have decent acting schools, but that's not their focus. All I've wanted to do my whole life is be an actress.

The door behind me opens.

"I think we're going to split the stage in half, at least initially."

I scoot down in my seat and hold my breath. It's Wes.

"When did you get into set design?"

With a *girl.*

"A couple of years ago I made a planetarium for a friend of mine. Taft saw it and asked me to start designing stuff for our plays."

"You built a *planetarium* for someone? That's so sweet."

Wow, I would have liked to see Wes make something like that. I wonder who he made it for, and part of me feels jealous that it wasn't for me.

He munches on an apple or something crunchy and they walk down the farthest aisle of the auditorium. I'm stuck in here now and there is no way in hell I'm letting them know I'm listening.

"That's where we're going to hang Titania's bower. Taft is nearly jumping up and down about that."

The girl giggles. I'd like to slap her. "What's a bower?" she asks, and I roll my eyes. Wes is too good for this girl. Their feet echo on the stage and Wes points at the ceiling.

"It's like a private room, but it's up in a tree." He laughs. "It sounds really stupid."

"She's a fairy?" she asks.

"Yeah, but a powerful one."

It's quiet for a second and I dare to scoot up in my seat to see what they are doing. The girl reaches for Wes's hand. She's tall with long blond hair, and I don't recognize her, even though I can't exactly see, as her face is cast in shadow. I have to press on the armrest to get a good look. My hand is still sore from the incident outside. Wes takes her hand and because it's only ghost lighting, it's all shadows when she leans into his chest. Their profiles are highlighted against the scenery, and I think they might kiss. My stomach clenches. His face is tilted down toward hers. Ugh, I can't look away.

Everything is copper in my mouth. I lean hard against the auditorium seats. It makes my skin burn, but I don't stop.

Their faces meet with a kiss, just for a moment, but the girl laughs, so they pull apart.

"Want to see the set designs?" he asks, and he leads the girl backstage. I know there is a door on the other side of the theater that lets out into the hallway, near the gym. Not even the auditorium is a safe place for me anymore.

I get up and walk to the double doors at the top of the auditorium aisle. Before I step outside, I run through the last few days with my old friends. I've been going about this *all* wrong. I've been asking May to tutor me, hitching rides from Panda, and saying weak hellos in the hallway. I've been being all awkward and sneaky.

I turn to the hazy lit stage. In my head I am on that stage as Beatrice, I am with my friends, laughing and horsing around during rehearsals. I don't know why I didn't think of doing this earlier.

I am going to try out for *Midsummer*. To hell with saying sorry every other minute if no one is going to forgive me. If they won't come to me—*fine.* I'll go to them.

I press my back against the auditorium door and enter the hallway. I stalk, as much as I can with a limp, down the hall, my jaw clenched. The buzz in my stomach keeps me going to Ms. Taft's office. I pass Kylie, Eve, Lila, and Tank in a small group by Kylie's locker.

I don't even look over.

"Penny, you okay?" Tank calls in his booming voice.

But I keep going around the corner.

There's usually a metal bin outside Taft's office with audition scripts, but it's empty now. I check the poster on the wall again—September 28th. That's tomorrow.

I knock on the door, but when I peek in the window, no one's at the desk. Damn it. I'll just have to try later in the day. With a glance down the hall, I see that Wes and the girl, who is nearly as tall as he is, are farther down the hallway. They turn a corner, I assume to walk to class. I want to know about Wes's life again. I hate that I'm jealous of her—I know him better than she does. And the only way I'm going to get near him with any kind of regularity is by doing what I love—acting.

I'm definitely coming back later.

Definitely.

I email Taft about getting a script for auditions, but when I check my phone on the way home from a neuro appointment after school, there's no word back. Bettie drives me home, and when she stops in the driveway there's another car I don't recognize next to my parents'. When I open the door, Mom's voice echoes from the living room. I check for Bettie but she's heading down the road.

"Well, you know, it's actually been quite difficult. Even though the Alice Berne name is on the banner of most of our events, and while I trust my team endlessly, I've missed being the commander in chief," Mom says.

I frown, stepping into the kitchen, catching the look on my face in the reflection of the oven. I shake my head to rid it of that terrible expression. Through the doorway and across the foyer is the living room, where a blond journalist nods. I think I've seen her before. She might be on TV but I can't be sure.

"But, you know," Mom says with an exaggerated sigh, "when the Cenberry family saw Penny's story run in the news last week, they contacted me yesterday to see how she was, and one thing led to another and they asked me to plan their daughter's two-million-dollar wedding. So it looks like I've been rehired."

I haven't heard Mom's business voice in a long time. A chill runs through me at her tone, and I press my back against the kitchen counter.

"Officially reinstated as commander in chief?" the journalist asks.

"Well, no, but I am in negotiations with my old team now."

"Who wouldn't take an opportunity like that?" the journalist asks, and there's the clink of glassware.

I check for bottles; I peek at the wine fridge too—it's still empty. Mom's good tea from France is on the counter. It's barely three thirty, but that's never stopped her before.

I back toward the kitchen door, the way I came in.

"Now, I didn't want to mention this, Mrs. Berne, but I think the readers of *Rhode Island Magazine* will want to know about your side of the Best Of Rhode Island incident and your twelve-week stay at the Bellevue Rehab Facility."

I grip the door handle. Rehab center?

"Of *course*," she says. "I am willing to admit that it was a very dark time for me."

"Is all of this—*in the past*?" the journalist says, speaking in a concerned saccharine whisper.

"Oh yes. I had some soul-searching to do."

"What about Penny? Has she helped you?"

"Oh, you know, she does. But Penny is . . . different. A dramatic child. She always loved the spotlight."

"Is she back in the theater?" the journalist adds. I make a closed fist around my house keys. I'm almost at the kitchen door.

Mom went to rehab. That's horrible.

"Alice!" Dad calls from the basement. "If you want to meet with Laney at the restaurant, you should go in fifteen minutes. I'm almost out the door myself!"

"Of course, dear!" Mom calls back.

Of course, dear?

Mom launches into an explanation of Dad's newest invention.

With my back against the kitchen door, I close my eyes and exhale. In the darkness behind my closed eyes, an image flashes:

I am gripping a cell phone. An empty wine bottle rolls across the kitchen floor.

I gasp and my eyes fly open to a flickering vanilla candle on the stove. The image sifts away so it's not as clear as it was a second ago. I know it's not entirely familiar, what I am seeing in my head, but I can still remember and *that's* something.

"Penny has shown real growth in the last year. Once she stopped acting, she became much more ambitious and serious about her studies. She was delightful onstage, such a star, but she's much more focused on her future now."

Yeah, I was in the library all the time to get away from you. The thought just rips through my head and I know it's absolutely true. If I was studying at Kylie's or in the library then I didn't have to be here.

My body seems to be reacting for my mind. I take out my cell and text Panda.

I'm going to try out for this play and not tell Mom a single thing.

Me: Where you at?

PANDA: Sev.

I edge the door closed behind me and step back outside.

My physical therapist would do leaps of happiness because I walk all the way to the 7-Eleven at the end of Cowesett Road, five whole blocks away. Despite the fact that the 7-Eleven claims to close at eleven, they actually close at twelve thirty. True to form, I find Panda smoking a cigarette outside.

He stands next to a picnic table with a group of guys I don't know very well, and when he sees me he waves and hangs up his cell phone. Richard sits in front of him at the table and leans on an elbow to speak more intently to Luke, one of the guys that hangs out in the computer lab a lot. I think he helped me with a document format one time freshman year. Through the smoke,

Panda waves me over. Once I step to his side, I can hear the conversation more clearly.

"I'm sorry but the special edition makes *sense*," Richard says. He has on a button-down shirt like usual. His thick-framed glasses are dark red today. I'm happy to see he still changes out his glasses all the time.

"Han wouldn't have shot Greedo," Panda says, and rests a hand on Richard's shoulder.

"Are you guys talking about . . . *Star Wars*?" I ask. At first, I think there are twinkle lights above the table, but it's dozens of fireflies batting about. Every once in a while someone has to swat a couple out of the way.

"Penny, Han Solo isn't a killer, he's got a conscience. Am I right?" Richard says, and I'm impressed he thinks I would know, which I do. Dad and I love those movies.

"He's a pirate," I say. "He's motivated by money."

This sends half of the table into an uproar and the other half applauds me. A guy I don't recognize says, "See! Even *Penny Berne* knows."

I bristle. Even *Penny* knows—a girl like *me*—whoever that is.

"'Smuggler' would be the appropriate term. Only Lando calls him a pirate," says Thomas Weston, a guy I knew in middle school. I'm pretty sure he's rolling a joint.

"You've walked into dangerous territory, Penny," Panda says.

"I actually came to talk to you," I say lightly, pulling at his T-shirt, which tonight has a logo of the Circle K convenience store on it.

"Moi?"

"Oui," I reply. "Want to get a Slurpee? My treat."

"Hey, Penny!" Thomas calls. I turn. "We heard you have some tattoos or something. From the strike." His eyes dart to his buddies at the table. Richard even twists to me. "Is it true?"

They don't seem grossed out and they aren't acting like Eve, who whispered about me when I walked by her today on the way to English class. Of course, Kylie said nothing in my defense. I push up one of the sleeves of my hoodie.

"They're called Lichtenberg figures," I say.

"It's fucked up," Richard whispers. "But they're awesome. What are they?"

As usual, I explain, "They're like bruises. From where the lightning hit the skin. They were supposed to go away right away, but they didn't. So I'm kind of a science experiment."

"Wild!" Thomas says. He had stood up to get a look at my skin, but sits back down.

"You're like a piece of art," Richard says.

I'm surprised how much I like the attention, but I came here for a purpose.

"Slurpee?" I say to Panda, and back away from the table.

As we head inside, Richard cries, "But if Han shoots first that makes him a cold-blooded killer!"

When we push inside, Carl, the manager, is counting money behind the counter.

"You kids need hobbies," he says, and glances up quickly.

"My hobby is my intellect, Carl. Hey, I'm auditioning for another play, you gonna come see it? Lord knows my own parents won't."

"Who says you'll get a part?"

"Oh come on, Carl. Have a little faith," Panda says with mock hurt.

Carl raises an eyebrow. "Is it going to be another musical? It took me a month to get *Oklahoma* out of my head. And then I saw that . . ." He snaps his fingers, searching for the word with a roll of his hand, except clenched in his fingers is a wad of twenty-dollar bills.

"Oedipus Rex," Panda fills in for him.

"Oh god. The chorus with the masks!" he cries. I didn't realize that Panda and Carl knew one another in any other way than just surly 7-Eleven owner and customer. But the way they are talking, Carl seems more like a friend, a coach. I wonder if it's because Panda's relationship with his parents has gotten even worse in the past year. I wish I could have been there for him more than just that one day with his dad. Maybe we all go through stuff we don't want other people to know about. I'm just glad he has Carl. Even if Carl is kind of a grouch.

"No masks," Panda says. "But it's Shakespeare! It's a classic."

"If the Lightning Strike Girl is in it," he grumbles, and motions to me, "maybe. You know, *if* I can clear my schedule."

"How did you . . ." I begin, but he nods to the newspapers lining the front of his counter. The local papers have had front-page stories about me for days.

"You're a gentleman and a scholar, Carl," Panda says, and follows me to the Slurpee machine. "And don't forget the recommendation you said you would write. For the job at OSTC this summer?"

"Only if you agree not to wear that T-shirt in here again," Carl grumbles, motioning to Panda's Circle K shirt. I bet he wore it just to annoy Carl.

"I asked you for a 7-Eleven T-shirt, but you still haven't delivered."

"Eleven ninety-nine," Carl says, and gestures to the T-shirts displayed on the wall.

"Come on, Carl! The rec! You already said yes."

"You know I will," he grumbles, and licks his fingers to start counting again.

"You old softy," he says, and follows me to the Slurpee machine.

Panda brings his hand to his chin and taps it with his index finger. "Hmmm," he says. "Decisions, decisions." I grab a medium cup and pour a Dr Pepper Slurpee.

"I would have pegged you for a Crystal Light girl," Panda says, and pours a Raspberry Slurpee.

"I think there's a lot you don't know about me," I say. "Maybe that's my fault."

"Oh, I'm willing to bet you're right," he says.

I'm looking at the Slurpee levers when I say, "I want to change. I'm trying. It's weird—not knowing who I've been. Maybe I've never been sure—even before the strike."

"I know, Berne," says Panda. "I told you. I'm here for you."

I pay for both of our Slurpees and we head outside. When I place my bag down, something catches Panda's eye. He uses his index finger to widen the front pocket of my bag and peer inside.

Then he slips out a pack of cigarettes.

"What?" I say, and pull out the little pocket to see inside, except it's empty. "I don't smoke. I've never smoked."

"Guess that's not true."

We sit down on the curb in front of the store. I want to know if he has any updates on May, but I don't want to sound like I only came here for information. I also want the script. I guess wanting things from people and not giving anything back makes you kind of a jerk. I don't have anything to offer him.

"For fuck's sake," Panda says. "At least give me a damn lighter if you're going to take forever to tell me what you came here for." He swipes my bag and roots around, pulling out a bright green lighter. "Don't look at me all surprised," he says. "It's *your* bag." I ran through the various times I had used the bag over the last week or so. I would never think that I would have cigarettes in my possession. I *hate* smoking.

"Keep it," I say, wondering how I even became a smoker in the first place. Gross.

I try to find a way to start this sure-to-be awkward conversation, and focus on the asphalt. Panda told me that morning he drove me to school that I keep my feelings from people. That I hide. I don't *feel* like I do. And if I do, I don't want to be that person anymore. "I was hoping you could make good on what you said," I finally say. "About helping me?"

"What's up?"

"I fell down in the cafeteria because I had a hand spasm, and May walked me down the hall. It was all sorts of awkward. Our tutoring session was . . . weird."

"Hey, who do you think convinced her to be your tutor?" He sips his Slurpee loudly and grins.

"You?"

"When the counselor asked her, she almost said no. I mean, she wanted to say no." My heart drops. I sort of imagined in my head that she said yes because deep down, May *wanted* to be my tutor.

"What? You have a look on your face," Panda says. "All I asked her was if the situation reversed, if she lost her memory and the only person she wanted to be with one-on-one was you, would she want you to show?"

I'm touched by his loyalty.

"I reminded her what you did for me too," he adds.

"I wish I could remember."

"You will, Berne," he says with a heavy exhale of cigarette smoke. I decide to tell Panda what I heard tonight in the kitchen. It's safe here with the fireflies and lazy traffic pulling up and down Cowesett Road.

"Did you know my mom went to rehab?" I try to read his expression.

"Yeah," he says. "Everyone knew. I don't think I ever heard you talk about it though."

"Was that why I quit theater?"

"I don't know why you quit. None of us do. I mean, we figured it had to do with your mom, but you wouldn't say anything. And I guess May tried to confront you for lying, but you blew her off. Kylie would tell off anyone who pushed you too hard about it. You weren't the most approachable I've ever seen you."

I shake my head at the parking lot and the endless number of fireflies in the air.

"What about Kylie? She said something about her car breaking down, but it doesn't explain the timeline."

Carl comes out of the Sev with a flyswatter.

"Damn bugs are a menace," he says, and bats at the fireflies.

"It's a fruitless endeavor," Panda says. He tries to capture a bug between his thumb and index finger but misses.

A Channel Six news van pulls into the lot and the driver gets out to walk into the Sev.

"Seeing a lot of those bastards driving around chasing the bug story," Panda says. "I heard my dad saying it. The two major universities are bringing in entomologists from all over the world."

I bat one out of the way that bobs between Panda and me.

When we're alone again, he says, "I guess you helped Kylie when her old Corolla broke down. After that, you guys hung out all the time. I saw you at Tank's parties. You guys wore each other's clothes—it was weird. It was like you changed overnight. You stopped being super outgoing. Quiet even."

"In that order?"

"Hell, I don't know!"

Carl knocks on the glass and motions for us to move.

"You love us, Carl!" Panda calls back. Carl rolls his eyes and goes back to cashing out the register. Instead, Panda lights up another cigarette.

"You were different all of a sudden," he says. "Callous. Kind of icy. And before, you were—" He looks me up and down. "Well, kind of like how you are now."

"Which is how?" I sit up straighter at this.

"Funny, loud, you're not afraid to jump into conversations. But you became really . . . weird. Like Kylie's icy, detached sidekick. You made fun of May at a party in front of Kylie's crew."

I put my face in my hands and groan.

"Why would I do that?"

"Look, forget it," Panda says, trying to backtrack. "Who needs details?"

"It doesn't even sound like me."

Panda exhales and says, "It felt like it *wasn't* you." He pauses.

"So why did you come out here tonight?" he asks. "Out with it." He's right. We won't solve anything trying to hash out details that neither of us know.

"I want to audition for *Midsummer*. I went to look for some scripts at the end of the day but there weren't any left in the bin. I even emailed Taft but she didn't write me back."

"Did you really think she would?"

"Well, yeah."

"You quit the play during tech week. She made you sit with the headmaster for two days and tried to convince you not to walk out on the play so close to performance. You crushed little Taft's heart."

I stand up, not wanting to hear any more. The urge to "fix my situation" overwhelms me as it has the last few days. Panda stands up too.

"I have to be in the play. It's the only way I can think of to prove to everyone I'm serious. Taft included. She sent me a card in the hospital. I think there's a chance she'll forgive me."

Panda reaches into his back pocket, pulling out the script for *Midsummer*. He hands it over.

"We're not auditioning for the mechanicals until after the weekend," he says. "Guess who I'm hoping for?"

"Bottom?" I say, speaking of the lovable character who is turned into a donkey.

"You know it," he says, and tosses his finished Slurpee into the trash.

"Thank you," I say, and hug Panda tight. I don't care that the figures still burn a little when he hugs me back. "And thank you for the card. The Flash. Lightning? I get it."

"Aw, Berne," he says while walking backward toward the picnic table. "You're still punny to me."

I laugh, which makes me want to hug him to me once more. I don't, though, I let him join his friends. I slip the script into my back pocket and start the long walk home.

THIRTEEN

AUDITIONS ARE MEANT TO START AT FOUR THIRTY. I stand just outside the double doors to the auditorium at three forty-five. Half an hour ago, the hall was noisy and packed. Now, it's completely silent as I work up the courage to go in early.

I don't care if I look overeager. I want Taft to know how serious I am about this. I spent all last night and today trying to memorize the scene I want to read for. It's one where I'm in a fight with my best friend. I didn't get to memorize all of the noble girls' lines, but I have some of the key ones down. I pull open the door and expect to see other people here as early as me. I'm alone. Honestly, I was hoping that Wes might be here, but the plus side is that I don't need to hide the limp. I'm also grateful for the carpeting. It's not like people won't know I'm here, but it helps to muffle the uneven clip of my footsteps. I make my way down the aisle and grab a seat in the front row. I know what it takes to audition. Pretend no one is watching you, take a breath, and be the character. Be someone else. It's something I've never had a problem with.

I keep going over the lines while I wait, and ten minutes later voices echo from backstage. I close the pages of my script as Ms. Taft, Panda, and Richard come out to center stage.

"Of course I want her to audition. Let's just see if she actually sho—" Taft pauses when she sees me. Her frizzy curls are backlit by the stage lights, and her eyebrows shoot up.

"Penny!" Richard cries. Both he and Panda run down the steps to the front row. "Fancy meeting you here," Richard says, sitting down on my left side. Panda scoots into the seat on my right, trailing the smell of salt and vinegar chips with him. Even though she's trying to hide it, Taft smiles when she sees me.

"I didn't expect to see you here," she says, and cocks her head just a little. "Good to have you back."

I meet her at the edge of the stage. She bends down to me.

"I emailed you for a script but Panda loaned me his."

"I heard," she says.

Behind me, the doors open and a handful of people come into the auditorium. They head down the center aisle and as the doors almost close, they open again. May, Karen, and Wes follow in a second group of people. We're almost all here—all my old friends.

"Can I audition?" I ask.

The tightness in my body makes my figures ache. I just want to sit down in the back of the room where it's dark.

"We'll need to talk," she says.

"Sure. I mean yes," I say.

"Which part are you auditioning for?" she asks.

"Helena or Hermia," I say, and she nods, making a note on a piece of paper. I'm going for the two leads—it's all or nothing.

"All right. Go ahead and take a seat." She eyes me warily.

I limp to a chair, making sure to use my left side to lower myself down.

Ms. Taft begins her speech about *Midsummer*, her intentions and plan for approach. Looks like we're doing it traditional, and even I have to chuckle with everyone else when there's a collective groan at this news.

Ms. Taft continues, "So we're going to design the stage so that we can move the trees to help dress either the woods or the city of Athens." Taft explains the duality of *Midsummer* and how the theme of opposites is explored in the contrast between the city and the forest settings. Even though I'm nervous, I love this part: the anticipation of sets to be built, the passion of believing in a character's story, and the rush of moving an audience to tears.

She explains the thematic importance of doubles and how the actress cast as Titania will also play Hippolyta and the actor cast as Theseus will play the fairy king Oberon as well. My shoulders ease for the first time in weeks. I *know* her voice, I *know* this place, and I know who to be.

A few rows ahead, Karen scribbles on a small pad. I should be taking notes or something. I want to dig in my bag for a pen but don't want to draw any more attention to myself.

"Okay, so everyone read over your lines one last time," Taft says, looking at her watch. "We'll get started in a few minutes."

I scoot down in the seat and read over the scene again. Okay, so this is the moment where Helena and Hermia are fighting because Lysander, Hermia's boyfriend, is under the influence of a love potion. He suddenly claims to love Helena, Hermia's best friend. Okay, I don't want to get confused as to who loves who, so I draw a little chart to get it straight. Classic love triangle. Demetrius is supposed to be with Helena and Lysander is supposed to be with Hermia but the love potion makes everyone love Helena. Got it.

"Okay, Penny and May, you'll go through this scene. Penny, why don't you try Helena, and May, I want to see you as Hermia. We'll just block it simply. In this scene, Helena, you don't believe that the guys, under the influence of the love potion, actually love you, and you're blaming your friend for planning this whole thing as a mean prank. So . . ." She looks to the script to decide. "Richard and Wes, you guys come up and remember, you're in love with Helena, so you want to be fighting it out in the background."

The theater springs into action. I recite Helena's lines under my breath as I walk to the stage. "I pray you, though you mock me, gentlemen, let her not hurt me!" I try a few different inflections as I walk to the stage.

We all gather in the center of the stage. The mood is serious—no one is laughing or joking like at the rehearsals I remember and I wonder if it's because of me.

Concentrate, Penny.

Find the emotion in the moment and make it realistic for yourself. It's almost too easy considering how angry May has been with me.

"Action!"

"You juggler! You canker blossom!" May yells at me, and the room erupts into laughter. "You thief of love!" She points at me with a sneer and we continue through the scene, making up the blocking as we go along. As we get to the end, we circle each other.

When Hermia jumps at me, I grab Wes's waist and hide behind him. It feels weird to touch him again like this. It used to be second nature to nudge him or push him or rest my head on his shoulder. Now, it's like I'm looking for permission.

I look down at my script and try to focus.

"You perhaps may think, because she is something lower than myself, that I can match her!" I cry.

"Lower! Hark, again!" May cries back.

Richard is trying not to laugh, but covers it up by shoving Wes, fighting for me.

I am supposed to be reasoning with Hermia, so I plead the line, "Do not be so bitter with me." But the next line after that is "I evermore did love you, Hermia." The idea of saying "I love you" to May trips me up. I miss my cue. May repeats her last line.

"Lower? Hark, again!"

Her face at the library was *so* angry. Not the theatrical sneer she has here, but true anger. The kind that makes people seem brittle and hard with the effort of containing it.

The back of my throat tickles like I'm about to cry.

"Good Hermia, do not be so bitter with me," I whisper. "I evermore did love you, Hermia." My voice cracks. A flush of heat sweeps my cheeks.

I hold in a sob and it makes my chest ache. I did love May. She was my best friend.

May breaks character and steps back from me. The way May looks at me, I feel like I'm on the verge of remembering something I'd buried. I clear my throat and continue, "Did ever keep your counsels . . ."

But none of that is true. I didn't keep her counsel; I made fun of her at a party. I kept secrets.

Ms. Taft and all the drama hopefuls watch me. I sniff, trying not to snot all over this audition.

"Never wronged you—" I say, and my bottom lip trembles. Because I know, in real life, I did.

Before me, standing in the center of the stage, are my friends, but they aren't. Not anymore.

A memory comes over me, so suddenly that I stumble:

May, Wes, and I lie on the center of the stage with an incredible constellation revolving on the ceiling above us. May loops her arm through mine and points at the revolving sky.

A hot tear rolls over my cheek and I quickly wipe it away.

I look down at the paper in my hand and read my line directly even though I have completely lost the character and the moment. The audience is silent.

"I mean—You see how simple?" My words come out thick.

"And how fond I am." The script hangs lifeless in my hand.

"That's great, guys," Taft says quickly. "That's all we need."

I pretend to itch my nose but wipe a few tears from my cheeks.

"That was great. Why don't we all take five?" She's completely lying. That wasn't great. I broke character and cried in the middle of my scene. I ruined the audition, my big chance to get back to the life I know.

All eyes in the audience are on me. Karen whispers something to Panda. I can't believe I came here. People get up and stretch, but I make my way toward the door before anyone can say anything. I press my fat, numb toes into the bottom of my shoes and exit out to the hallway.

When I get outside to the parking lot, the rush of the audition scene ripples away into the early evening air. Mom and Dad are both out at work events, and the doctors say I'm still not allowed to drive on my own. That's right—I'm stuck here. I dial Bettie's number; it rings three times before she answers. I ask her to come early.

"I can't get there until seven, hon," she says. I check my phone. It's only five o'clock. "I'm waiting with Maddie to finish up her dentist appointment." Maddie is her youngest daughter.

"It's no problem," I say. "I'll be waiting out front."

She promises to try to get here as soon as she can. Regardless of what happens, I'm not going back in there. I'll just find another way to get my old life back.

I sit down on the curb and watch the fireflies weave through the parking lot. Thirty-six more hours . . . just thirty-six until I can "technically" drive again.

* * *

About a half hour later, I get a text. As I reach to take out my cell phone, I realize something: my mouth tastes totally normal. No weird metallic taste. I want to jump for joy. Then I see the text from Bettie.

BETTIE: Looks like the dentist can't see us until 6—don't want to make you sit any longer than you need. Can you get a ride from one of your friends?

Crap. Auditions are still going on, and I can't go back inside after that embarrassing performance.

I run through my options and scroll through my phone contacts—it strikes me now that I haven't done that yet. Lila, Eve, and Tank Anderson—I have *all* their numbers; they must have transferred automatically from my old phone. Technically we're friends, so why do I feel like I can't call them?

In a cruel moment of serendipity, the door behind me opens and Wes comes outside with his sketchbook under his arm.

I immediately hold my breath, smooth my leggings, and run a finger under my eyes to make sure my mascara isn't smeared from crying. Wes walks to the first line of cars and stops at a black Mustang. It's an older style but it's sleek. What happened to the ancient minivan? He unlocks the car as I pretend to scroll through my phone. There's a clank of keys as he sighs and his shoulders drop.

"Penny?" he says.

"Hey, yeah," I say, and stand up. I walk toward his car. It's useless to pretend I don't want or need a ride at this point. This might even distract him from my super awesome audition.

"What are you still doing out here?"

"Just waiting for a ride," I say, but it takes me like four times to get the damn sentence out. I hate that I trip over my words.

His face softens, a little.

"You stutter when you're nervous, Berne. Good to see some things haven't changed."

I manage a grin.

"I'm not allowed to drive until the end of the week. I've already had a shitty afternoon. Come on, don't make me say it."

He seems like a stranger with his hand on the car door—he's actually debating if he should help me out or not.

"Fine," I say with a sigh. "Wes, will you drive me home in your very fancy car which is not your mom's minivan?"

I note that even though he looks away from me, he smiles.

"Come on," he finally says, and opens the passenger door for me.

There are discarded sketches, coffee mugs, and old candy wrappers scattered across the floor of the black Mustang. I see one sketch that looks a little like a tree for the *Midsummer* set, but not quite. My heart leaps as I realize what it looks like: the vines and branches that crawl across my stomach. The ones Wes saw the other day in the hall. I hope that it's not just a coincidence. We are silent as we drive out of the school parking lot and onto the road. The whole car smells like wood chips and sawdust.

I check him out as casually as I can. Wes has left just one too many buttons undone at the top of his shirt. It looks good. Kind of sexy.

He glances over at me and I jump into a conversation. I pick up one of the sketches from the floor.

"You've gotten really good," I say. "Um, stop me if I've already told you that, and forgot it along with everything else."

"You haven't," he says. I can't read his tone, but he lightly takes the sketch from my hand and tosses it into the backseat.

"Guess you don't want me to look at that?"

"It's just a sketch for *Midsummer*. It's no big deal."

He licks his lips, which *I* know he does when *he's* nervous. Busted. It makes me feel a little better.

"Have you been doing a lot of the sets?" I ask.

In the amber light of the night falling over the sky, I can see that he's got some scruff that lines his jaw and cheek, like a beard he's not letting grow all the way in. It looks good on him. A lot has changed since we were friends. He swipes some of the blond hair out of his eyes.

"I've been into woodworking more than drawing," he says. It's hard to concentrate on what he's saying, though, because a rush of thoughts enters my head. No wonder I felt a little awkward grabbing onto him today at auditions. I *know* it suddenly without being able to explain it. Wes was always my best friend, but I *think* we were something more. It makes sense why he could barely look at me in the hallway with my stomach exposed. Now I can't help staring at his mouth. A desire to kiss him overwhelms me. "I made the backdrop for *Into the Woods*," he says. I snap out of my reverie.

"We did *Into the Woods*?! I *hate* that play!" I cry.

"I know," Wes says with a laugh. "We all did. But Taft was really excited about it." His smile is so familiar, like he's got a small joke he's keeping from me, and for a split second it feels like nothing has changed. But as quickly as it came, his smile falls again.

"Anyway, Taft liked my designs," he finishes. "So I got to do some stuff for OSTC this summer. They paid me a thousand bucks."

"Wow!"

With my left hand, I grip the armrest and rub my thumb against it nervously. I wish I had been there to see it. Instead, all I can manage to add is, "That's cool," and I want to smack myself.

"How's your hand?" he asks. The memory of having the spasm by the tables in the outside caf replays in my head. I cringe.

"You heard about that?"

"Not in a bad way," he says quickly, and I appreciate that he's trying to make me feel better. "Just that it . . ." He seems to choose his words. "That you were in pain."

"It can happen when I move too fast," I explain. "It's part of recovery, apparently. It should stop soon. It's not supposed to last, anyway."

I notice more about Wes as we turn onto my street and pass under the streetlamps: the frayed jeans and the black duct tape covering the top of one of his boots. He's turned into such a theater techie.

"You're different," I say.

He pulls up to the end of my driveway.

"Should I walk you in?" he asks, ignoring my comment. He coughs awkwardly, and I realize that he is really asking if I need help walking. He stops the car, but I don't want to get out.

"I'll be okay," I say quietly. "Thanks for the ride."

I open the door, but before I'm even out of the car Wes's door slams, and he's helping me out. I know he's only worried I'll fall down. Once I'm upright, I hesitate with my hand on the doorframe. Ahead, in the woods that surrounds the houses, pulses of light, the fireflies, dance in the shadows by the thousands.

"Look," I say, and gesture with my chin. Wes turns. "I think there's even *more* of them now."

"I thought it was just media hype at first," he says, and shuts the door for me. It's unmistakable. Thousands of tiny glowing, yellow dots bob in the twilight. "They're kind of cool."

We walk up the drive in silence. Then Wes says, "I didn't know what to say, when you called me from the hospital. I'm sorry I didn't call you back."

"I didn't know what to say either."

"It must be really weird."

We're almost near the end of the driveway.

"It is. Sometimes think I know myself. I think for one split second that I know exactly who I am. Then someone tells me something or shows me a picture from a life that I just don't remember. I'm not even sure which version of me is the right one."

"Do you have to pick?" he asks.

"I don't know anymore. My parents talk to me like I'm split in two. Like there's an old version of me and a new version. Which I guess there kind of is. I just want to feel like me, whoever that is."

"How is your mom?" Wes asks. "You know, since rehab." It's

so weird that he *knows* about Mom in rehab, but I don't.

"I haven't seen her drinking too much," I say. "She's better now that the reporters have shown up and her company is courting her with big paychecks."

"That's good," Wes says, and we make it to the part of the driveway where the stone tiles curve around the house to the screened-in porch. "Maybe she's really different."

"I think maybe she is."

We share a small smile, and the only sound I hear is our footsteps.

"You seem different too," Wes finally says. "Even if you're split in two. Penny, you don't have to be a certain way just because people tell you that's who you are. You don't have to listen to them."

"Well." I fidget. "Maybe you can help me. Figure it out. Remind me."

"I'd like that," he says.

My left leg aches so I take a second to lean on the hood of Mom's car. I can sense the heat from the engine. I glance up at the house, but the lights are out. Good, Mom must be upstairs already.

Wes's eyes widen at something beyond me on the grass.

"Oh my god!"

He runs toward a figure lying on the grass.

Oh *no*. Something dark tugs at my memory. My stomach seizes. I want to race after Wes but can't. I'm messier when I'm trying to move quickly.

"Wait!" I call. "Wait!"

Wes stops short in the grass, making the car keys in his pocket jangle loudly.

I freeze next to him, trying to put together who I am seeing and what it means.

Mom lies on her side, her black hair framing her face. The cream-colored sweater she wears contrasts sharply against the bright green grass. Ropes pull at my stomach from each side in an invisible tug-of-war. I reach for Wes's arm and our skin touches, finally. He looks back to me; his eyes soften.

"Your mom—" he starts to say but doesn't finish. I don't want to know what he would have said.

"This is the first time I've seen her like this since I've been back," I say.

"You've seen her like this before?"

"In tenth grade. Just before *Much Ado* auditions. It was really bad then."

An understanding passes over his features and he nods.

Wes squats to be closer to Mom. She sleeps in the fetal position. The lawn hose runs next to her, bubbling water onto the base of the hydrangea plants and pooling in the grass.

I walk to the side of the house, squeeze between some other hydrangeas, and turn off the valve. When I come back, Wes is checking Mom's pulse. She snorts, and he stands quickly.

"Well," he says. "Shit. What do we do now?"

Wes frowns at the ground, at Mom sleeping, and the shiny pool of water drowning the grass. Fireflies pulse around us, but even though I am in the yard, I stand in the center of a stage, a spotlight on me. My cheeks burn, rooting me to my body and the ground where my mother remains passed out. The way her face is positioned on the grass, the skin of her cheek pulls down, making it seem as though it sags when it doesn't naturally.

"She was doing so much better," I whisper. "I don't know what . . ." I search for the reason. It's sick but in a weird way I almost wish she had tripped or fallen or hurt herself. It would be a better reason for lying here than being too drunk to walk ten feet to the house.

"Where's your dad?" Wes whispers. He can talk in his normal voice, she's out, but he speaks softly anyway.

"He's in Boston for a dinner meeting." I look down at my right foot. "I have to get her inside," I say.

"You think *you're* getting her inside? Penny, I've seen you at school since the strike. You can only carry two books at a time. Your textbook and some journal thing."

"Please, Wes, just go. I'm already completely humiliated."

Being out here with Wes and the moonlight, and the beautiful fireflies, should have been an important moment. It should have been special. Instead, it's all about Mom.

Wes lifts Mom under her arms so her back rests against his chest. He lifts her enough so that her heels don't scrape against the ground, and carries her the rest of the way down the stone path toward the house. I open the door for them, and help them onto the screened-in porch.

"Put me dowwwn," Mom groans. "I'm sleeping."

I grab an extra pillow from the porch swing and place it under Mom's head, as Wes lays her lengthwise on the couch. Thank god she's wearing black dress pants and not a skirt. I pull her sweater down a little so it doesn't rise up and show her stomach.

She snorts again and rolls into a fetal position. Truthfully, since the strike, I've forgotten about these nights. My head has been so full with everything else. I had just been so happy that she was better. Maybe I saw it because I wanted it to be true.

Mom tucks her hands under her cheek and curls her knees in to her belly. Good. If she's on her side I don't have to sleep out here and watch her. We learned in health class that drunk people can choke on their own vomit if they sleep on their backs. The one thing I learned in that class that applied to my actual life.

"I can bring her inside," he whispers. I am grateful that the moonlight shines onto the floor, hiding my face. I don't want to make eye contact right now.

I cross my arms over my chest.

"No, it's best if I let her think she chose to be out here."

I bring my hands up to cover my face.

"I am so sorry," I say, and I've never meant anything more. "Sorry for everything. For this, and for ignoring you, and even the things I don't remember. I was horrible."

"You're not horrible," he says after a pause that takes too long.

His features are hard and chiseled, yet the look in his eyes is soft. He has a face of contradictions. I miss him and he's standing right in front of me.

A tremble runs through me.

"You're shaking," he says, and the concern in his voice makes me shudder again. I can tell he wants to say something else. He opens his mouth but then closes it quickly.

"I should go," he says, and in the silence that follows, we both know that's not what he wanted to say.

We walk back to his car at the same pace, even though I'm being slow. The fireflies pop in and out of the darkness in a syncopation of light.

"Want me to stay to make sure she's okay?" he asks, and bends down to grab something from the driveway. It's the bag that I brought with me to auditions. The journal has slipped out, along with my brush and makeup case. He picks them up and hands back the journal last.

"What are you always scribbling in this thing?"

He's already seen the truth of my life, seen my crying at auditions. I don't *want* to hide anything from Wes ever again. I flip through the entries and show him what I have so far. I show him the hospital bracelet and Panda's card. Tonight I'll add the memory I had earlier, about the constellations in the theater. It will help if I have it written down so I can reference it if and when more of my memories return.

He leans over to get a better look at the book and I inhale his scent; a sweet but woodsy smell that I can't quite identify. My whole body hums. I want him to tell me that he misses me as much as I miss him—that he misses our jokes and our friendship. He leans on the back of Mom's old Lexus, my car, and crosses one ankle over the other. I pick one of Mom's hydrangeas from a flowering bush when he asks, "Have you been able to piece anything together?"

"Some." I gesture to the journal. "I paste in important documents or items like my hospital bracelet. Sometimes I just scribble stuff down. Like today at auditions." I decide to be daring again. "I remembered something—or, I think I did. And I wrote it down."

"What?"

I inhale slowly. "We were lying on our backs on the stage. The ceiling was a constellation of stars."

He looks at me sharply. "You remembered this?"

"Yeah," I spin the hydrangea flower nervously between my fingers. "But that couldn't be a real memory, right? How could there be stars on the ceiling of the theater?"

Wes gives me a strange look. Then he gets into the Mustang without another word.

"What did I say?" I call after him.

The car engine revs and he pulls out of the driveway so fast that dust kicks up around the tires.

"Wes! Wait!" I cry, but he doesn't stop.

I watch the red taillights as they burn through the blackness at the end of the street and pull away.

FOURTEEN

LATER THAT NIGHT, I'M HALFWAY THROUGH revising my English paper on *Beowulf*. I would have been done hours ago but I keep getting distracted, alternating between thinking about Wes and checking in on Mom. The look on Wes's face keeps running through my head. Finally, around 11:30, Mom moved herself from the porch to her bed, and I could finally stop worrying and concentrate.

Now, I replay the awful moment when Wes got into his car like it's a video on loop—*you remembered this?*—when there's a knock on my patio door.

My room has two doors, one that leads to the rest of the house, and one that leads to an outside landing with a staircase going down to the driveway. Only two people ever use that entrance, and one of them couldn't get away from me fast enough earlier.

I have to squint, but when I flip on the outside light May stands on the landing, batting fireflies out of her face. This is where she used to always come in the house whenever it was past "appropriate hours." The door is locked, but she tries the knob. She's in pajama bottoms and an EG Private T-shirt.

I unlock the door and she bursts inside, her arms crossed over her chest. "In light of your emotional outburst at auditions, I've been doing some thinking. Here are the terms of our *relationship*."

I jump on my friend, holding her close to me, and squeezing tight.

"Can't breathe!" she squeals.

"Sorry!" I say quickly, and pull away. May tucks her long black hair behind her ears. I wonder if she's here because Wes told her about Mom's lovely show on the lawn tonight, but then I stop myself. It doesn't matter why May's here. I'm just glad she is.

"The terms are this," she says. "Complete and total honesty."

"I promise," I say.

She paces my room, ticking things off on her fingers.

"No more bullshit. You tell me when something is wrong. Don't shut me out."

I salute.

"Now close that door, because you're about to have a lightning bug colony take up residence in your bedroom," she says, and I rush to close the door behind her. A handful of fireflies are already bobbing around the ceiling.

May looks about the room. "It looks the same," she says, "except . . ."

"What?"

"It's gone," she says, and gestures to the window, empty except for dots of light from the fireflies outside.

In a flash—I see a ghost of a memory—May and I work together to hang a mobile made from geode slices, right there in the center window.

"The mobile," I say. "That's right. It was my fourteenth birthday. You helped me put it up." I can't help but smile. "I looked for it, when I got home from the hospital. I can't find it, though." May is not smiling, so I add quickly, "Who knows what pre-lightning Penny did with it."

She nods and sits down on the edge of my bed.

"I'm glad you came," I say, and sit down on my desk chair. "And don't worry, my mom hauled herself inside about an hour ago."

"From where?" May says, but I can tell she's playing dumb.

"Come on," I say with a raise of an eyebrow. "I know Wes told you."

May frowns. "Okay, maybe."

This is my chance.

"May," I say quietly. "What happened?"

"I only know my side of the story," she says. But she talks, tells me everything—all the things I haven't been able to remember for myself. The party when I made fun of her—the day I quit the play, and the expression on my face. That she had to find out about her best friend's mom going to rehab from the Channel Six news.

She fiddles with the blanket she's sitting on. "I know you probably threw out my mobile," she says. "Does that mean you also threw out the planetarium Wes made you?"

Wait. "What? He made *me* the planetarium?"

She tells me Wes spent nearly eighteen hours making a revolving star light show for me. It makes so much sense now why Wes freaked out when I brought it up.

"Why would he do that?" I breathe.

"Penny," May says with a familiar raise of her eyebrow. "Wes loved you. He'd always loved you. You broke his heart."

Wes *loved* me?

"Come on, he can barely look at you now. He was seeing some girl. Sabrina something? He ended it the other day. We all know why."

We talk for a couple of hours. At two in the morning, we're still sitting in my window seat with steaming hot mugs of tea. May let me go down on my own in case Mom got up.

"I forgot how much I missed London Fogs," I say.

"That's one thing I thought you'd *never* forget."

The fireflies dot the night sky by the hundreds. They make it seem like the stars are lower tonight, strewn about in the green foliage instead of the sky. "It's weird though," May continues. Her eyes seem pensive. "What you're blocking out."

"Blocking out?" I say.

"Well, it's just the last year or so—you know? Maybe it's . . ." She searches for the right word. "Denial?"

"Maybe," I say, and take a deep breath. "But I'm getting some of my life back." I smile a little at my best friend. "So maybe that's a good start." We clink mugs.

"I should go to bed," May says, and gets up to go.

"I'm sorry about my—" I say, intending to rehash it all again, but May holds up her hand.

"You can't keep apologizing, Pen." She is about to descend down the patio stairs when she turns to me. "It wasn't just what Wes told me tonight about your mom. I knew at auditions."

"What?"

"That you were still you."

She offers to pick me up in the morning to drive to school. Even though it's now less than thirty-six hours until I can drive again, I've never been happier to say yes.

The next morning, I text May and tell her *I'm* going to drive us.

"I'm feeling brave," I say when I get to her house. "I didn't want to wait."

"Reckless would be more accurate," she replies.

"Maybe driving will help jog my memories."

I haven't been back in this car since before the strike; the evidence of my old life is overwhelming. Coffee cups with names scrawled in messy barista handwriting litter the passenger-side floor: Lila, Eve, Kylie. I turn the ignition and my hand reaches instinctively for the gearshift. I press on the gas too hard and we lurch in reverse, sending cups flying. I slam on the brakes and the glove box flies open, spilling papers, mouthwash, and a strange tangle of plastic string and geode slices.

May leans forward, picking it up from the floor. I note her foot is crushing one of Kylie's old coffee cups.

"It's my mobile," she says, delicately untangling the many strings and geode slice ornaments. The morning sunlight makes the four crystals glint golden and silver light in the palm of her hand. It used to make little rainbows all over my bedroom floor. There are no rainbows at my feet now, just the coffee cups and discarded college brochures. I don't have any idea why it's shoved in my glove box. Once it's untangled she leaves it in her lap.

"I can totally cry again, if you want," I say, and she can't help laughing.

"Just don't kill us on the way to school, okay?"

We pull into the parking lot around 7:20 with fifteen minutes until homeroom. Except, when May and I get to the senior lot, there are three news trucks up near the entrance to school and people are swarming outside the double doors. Fireflies bob and weave between them, looking strange and surreal in the morning light.

May and I share a frown and get our school bags.

"What's going on?" we say at the same time.

I zip up my light jacket, happy to have another layer between the Lichtenberg figures and the news trucks. We walk up to find Panda, Richard, and Karen at the outskirts of the crowd. Panda's eating from a bag of barbeque chips and sitting on the hood of Richard's ancient SUV.

I can't help but notice that across the lot, Kylie consoles Tank by rubbing his back. In her other hand is a to-go coffee cup. I recognize the familiar barista's scrawl on the side. Her long braids are hidden under a baseball hat with the band name NIRVANA on the front in white block lettering.

"I am so tired of this town." I hear Kylie's voice in the back of my mind. I hesitate and bring a hand to my temple.

A memory! When did I hear her say that?

"What's happening?" May asks Panda, and I blink and turn back to the group.

"They have to cancel the football season." Richard grabs a chip from Panda's bag. "We're like totally devastated," he deadpans, and pretends to flip his hair over his shoulder in a pretty spot-on imitation of Kylie.

"Why?" I ask, and am surprised how much I care. I know that Tank will be disappointed. All three of them look to me. "Well." I shrug. "I mean, it's a big deal. They've never done that before." I care because something *else* is bleeding through. Tank will be devastated and I feel genuinely sorry for him.

I want to find out what's going on. I squeeze through some of the crowd. People stand behind the news anchors so they can wave at the cameras. One of the journalists looks familiar—she's the blond chick from my house who interviewed Mom! She's in a bright pink suit and holding the microphone in front of one of the science teachers, Mr. Pierce.

"Well, it's unprecedented," he says, and a firefly lands on top of his head. "But for the safety of our students and for the protection of the insects themselves, we will temporarily cancel our football season until the fireflies clear."

Alex James lifts up his shirt and jumps behind Mr. Pierce, dancing around like he's got a huge Hula-Hoop around his waist.

"You!" Headmaster Lewis cries, pointing a long finger at Alex. "My office!"

"They should migrate or die out once the first frost hits," Mr. Pierce explains over the spectacle as Alex is led into school.

The journalist turns to the camera.

"Just more fallout from these light-bearing insects that have inundated our little town. Reporting from EG Private, I'm Carolyn Norris for Channel Six News." Once the red indicator light on the camera goes out, the students disperse just as our first bell rings. We have five minutes to get to homeroom. The journalist is turning my way. A dash of panic runs through me.

I bend over and scoot toward the doors. The crowd is still pretty thick so I can hide.

"What the hell is Penny doing?" I hear May ask with a laugh.

I scoot into school undetected, surrounded by my classmates, all grumbling about the fireflies, which only a few weeks ago seemed so magical, so strange.

In homeroom, I'm finalizing my checklist for college applications when the morning announcements come over the loudspeaker.

"Sally Renson here. Homecoming is just over a week away and since we're all disappointed about football, make sure to show your school spirit and wear your school colors to our pep rally this Friday!"

"Whoop-dee-doo," a girl drawls from the back of the room. Everyone laughs but the room goes silent quickly at the next announcement:

"In true EG Private tradition, the top three homecoming nominees are automatically the members of the homecoming court. The results are finally tallied. But first our word of the day! Lampyridae," she says. "The scientific name of the *lightning bug.*"

A chorus of groans echoes in the room and even Ms. Reley, at her desk, laughs with us. We have to listen to a few minutes about the Latin origins of the word "Lampyridae," before Sally Renson finally gets to the announcement everyone is dying to hear:

"And now your homecoming court!"

Whoops and cheers echo down the hall from other homerooms, even though it's loud in here too. The girl on the loudspeaker reads the names of the guys in homecoming court, two whose names I recognize: Alex James and Greg Anderson, or "Tank," as we know and love him. There's also someone named Kurt Leonard. The homecoming queen is going to be obvious. There were dozens of nominees—hell, even I was nominated before the strike.

"The final three nominees for homecoming queen are: Kylie Castelli, Angela Wilson, and Penny Berne."

People squeeze my shoulder. Some pat me on the back—they whoop and cheer my name, and it all seems so silly. I say thank you, as I should, but I really, *really* don't want to be homecoming queen. There's more yelling and cheers out in the hallway. Even Ms. Reley congratulates me as I close up my planner and head out of the room.

"Penny!" May cries, running up to me after homeroom. "You never told me you were nominated."

"You mean you didn't run to the original nominations list and check the other twenty names weeks ago? I only know because Lila and Eve texted me when I was in the hospital."

"I didn't even vote," she confesses. "Come on, aren't you the least bit excited?" May asks, and loops her arm through mine.

"I'm blocking it out."

I hitch my books closer as we make our way down the hall, me toward marine biology, or science, and May to AP chemistry. I'd be going that way too, if not for the accident.

"And no, I'm not excited," I say, and mean it. "You know I was only nominated for one reason."

"And what's that?"

I go silent as we pass by Kylie, Lila, and Eve putting up a poster by one of the girls' bathrooms. It's a campaign poster. I pause at the picture she has chosen. I know it because I've seen it a zillion times online. Except, for this poster, I have been edited out—on purpose. It looks like Kylie, Lila, and Eve are standing, just the three of them, in a sea of people on the dance floor at the Joint, a local live music club that Kylie likes. In the original picture, I was right there next to Eve, her arm around my waist, but I've been digitally taken out of the picture. When I got home from the hospital, it had been taped up on my mirror. Now it sits in a pile on my dresser with other artifacts from a life I can't remember.

Kylie meets my eyes as we pass, but raises her chin. "Come on," she says. "Let's hang the rest of these. Some of us aren't getting pity votes."

It feels like a kick to the gut.

"Nice, Castelli," May says. "You're a real gem of a person."

"Mind your own business," she snaps back. "You've got your bestie back."

"Don't let her bother you," May says quietly, linking her arm tighter through mine. I wince at the pressure on the figures. They've definitely eased but they're still there and they still hurt.

You've got your bestie back.

I fight with myself to turn around and see if Kylie is watching us walk away.

"She is so petty," May says, and we turn into the hallway with the science classrooms. I tell May that I agree even though something in my gut tells me that she is wrong about Kylie.

As we walk, streamers hang in blue and gold from the ceiling; the school colors. Homecoming posters and pep rally reminders cover nearly every inch of the wall. But new posters, official school posters, have come up as well: FIREFLY SAFETY TIPS, followed by long lists of how we should close doors, turn off unnecessary outside lights, and do more to help hinder the "spread of the bug population."

We have to walk through the hall where the woodworking studios are to get to the science labs and classrooms on the second floor, in the new wing of the building.

"You successfully dodged my question about homecoming," May says. "I thought you were supposed to be getting better at that, per our agreement." She raises an eyebrow. "Why do you think you were nominated?"

I shrug. "You heard Kylie. People feel sorry for me."

"Maybe," she says, "but that seems kind of convenient. People like you. They always have. You were always fun to be around, always the life of the party. Even when you were going through your *Mean Girls*, *Invasion of the Body Snatchers* phase."

I nudge her. "Stop."

She laughs. "Sorry, but I don't think you should just assume that people are pitying you."

We stop outside one of the woodworking rooms. I peek in the door. It's Wes. He's standing in the middle of the room, surrounded by a forest made of wood. Tall wooden trees tower over him, with branches stretching out in all directions. It takes me a second before it clicks: they look like the sketches of my Lichtenburg figures that I saw in Wes's car. They're a beech wood, light in color, and unfinished.

"I'll see you at lunch," May says with a grin, and keeps walking down the hall. I'm going to be late to class, but I don't care. I knock but Wes doesn't seem to hear over the noise of the handsaw. He puts it down and runs a sander along one of the tree trunks. I step inside and hesitate.

"I didn't know you could do that," I say. Wes yelps, jumping back.

"Penny." He's breathless. "You scared me. I almost dropped the sander on my foot."

"I tried knocking, but you were in the middle of . . . all that."

His face softens. A few fireflies dart around the room; it's hard to see their pulsating lights under the bright fluorescent school bulbs. Wes follows my eyes.

"They're everywhere," he says. "During the day too."

"Did you see the news trucks outside the school this morning?" I say, and I'm grateful we can make small talk about something going on that's weirder than being struck by lightning and not remembering a whole year of your life.

I walk among the trees he's built.

"These are amazing," I say.

"Thanks," Wes says, and shoves his hands in his pockets. "Aren't you going to be late for class?"

"Aren't you?"

He raises an eyebrow. "I have a free period," he says. He smiles just enough so the corner of his mouth lifts. A warmth spreads through me from my belly up to my chest. Wes uses a regular piece of sandpaper and his muscles strain as he pushes it against one of the branches. My heart betrays me. The damn thing slams. Longing feels like an old wound that's been reopened, just below the solar plexus.

Could what May told me be true? That he loved me, and I broke his heart?

I guess he's not going to bring up what happened the other night with my mom. It felt like we got somewhere closer, a place I could understand, and a place that I knew. Wes continues to work. I can't help myself.

"Thank you," I say. "For my mom. For what you did."

He doesn't say anything but keeps sanding. Maybe I just have to let it go. Maybe I've gotten May back in my life and that needs to be enough. I turn to leave when Wes says, "Homecoming nomination, huh?"

"Yeah." I grin. "You should probably bow before me."

Wes laughs. "Don't push your luck, dollface." A rush rolls over me. A memory whispers at me in the back of my mind. I see Wes in my head in a white tunic and I know with certainty that this memory is from a rehearsal of *Much Ado*.

"Toots?" I say, and Wes pulls back.

"Honey?" he says.

"You're lucky you have access to power tools or I'd challenge you to a duel."

"Do you remember?" he adds, and doesn't respond to my jab. "That day?"

He holds my eyes and the whisper of the memory evaporates as fast as it came.

"Not the whole thing."

His eyes drop to my covered arms but he quickly busies himself with the last couple of tools and scattered pieces of sandpaper. He cleans up and it looks like he is heading out. If he asked, I would show him the figures.

"Are you going to the homecoming dance?" I ask, and the question has left my lips before I can think through if I should even be asking it.

"Oh, um." Wes fumbles. "Yeah."

"With that girl I saw you with the other day?" I know I'm fishing. Even though May told me he ended it, I want to hear it from him.

"Who?" he asks, and replaces the tool in a plastic safety box.

I try to be very casual. "You know, blond. Tall. Annoyingly high voice."

Wes grins. "Were you spying on me, Berne?"

"What! No." Busted.

He shakes his head and grabs his book bag. "No," he says with emphasis and joins me at the door—we're so close our shoulders touch. "She told me she thought theater was boring."

"Ouch," I say. "You need better taste, Gumby." He smiles but it's not to my face. He sticks his hands in his pockets. We hesitate, shoulder to shoulder at the door—only inches apart.

"You aren't her," he whispers, and it feels like we're talking about something else entirely. It takes me a second to catch up.

"What?"

"You're not your mom. You know that, right? I need you to know. I didn't mean it."

"Why do you sound like you're apologizing?"

He doesn't say anything else, but leaves the studio and lumbers, calmly, down the hall. Like the other night, I feel like I'm chipping away at the ice around him, though I can't be sure. Before I walk away, he glances back and I nearly call out to him. He nods just once before turning the corner.

A week later, when I'm about to lose my patience waiting for the cast list, someone screams just outside my math class. "The cast list is up!" I'm almost positive it's Karen.

I grab my books and limp to the door.

"Penny," my teacher, Mr. McKenney, says, "class isn't over."

I survey the dozens of eyes watching me and grip my books tighter. People are packing up because no matter how much Mr. McKenney wishes we could stay beyond class time, it's ridiculous. As I am about to make an excuse, the bell rings. He rolls his eyes and I head out to the hallway as quickly as I can, past the stage entrance to the auditorium, the radio broadcasting center, and finally the theater department office. A huge crowd has circled outside the bulletin board. I think I see May's black hair in the middle of the group.

"Yes!" she cries with a jump. "I'm Helena!"

I could still be Hermia. Maybe Taft gave me the other noble part.

Richard sprints by and jumps at the edge of the crowd, trying to see over their heads.

"Will you bastards *move*!" he cries. "Who am I, May?" he calls.

"Puck!" May's high voice calls back. She moves through the crowd and jumps into his arms. He swings her around and around in his purple button-down shirt and jeans. "I knew you would get it!" she cries.

"What *fools* these mortals be!" Richard's great stage voice echoes over the din of the hallway as he recites Puck's famous line. When he places her on the ground, May sees me, and her smile cracks just a bit. Disappointment hits me square in the chest. I had to expect that Taft wouldn't give me a lead role after what happened. Definitely not. Still, I'd been holding out hope.

"I didn't get a part, did I?" I say once I get close to them.

"Of course you did," she says, and it's too chipper, too high. She's out of breath. "You're Hippolyta."

"I am?" My heart soars. Taft let me in. I'm back. And I get to play the fairy queen! "So I'm Titania too, right? Taft said she would be using doubles for the roles of the human queen and the fairy queen. You know? To connect to the idea of opposites—city versus forest, yadda, yadda."

May shakes her head. "It just says Hippolyta. Karen got Titania."

"Oh," I say, and now I'm the one whose voice is way high.

"That's awesome." I know that Taft split up the parts when that wasn't her original vision. I'm not trusted to stick it out; why would she give me such a huge part?

"One more thing," May says, and I notice the crowd is thinning out behind her.

"What?" I ask with a grimace. "Do I want to know?"

"There's an asterisk next to your name."

"What?"

"You should go talk to her," Richard says.

I squeeze through a couple of people—one girl is crying because she didn't get a part at all—and I do see a small blue asterisk next to my name. I look to the bottom of the list and an asterisk is there too, with the line: *See Ms. Taft ASAP for further instruction BEFORE rehearsal begins.* I am the only one with an asterisk.

I rejoin my friends in the hallway as Panda struts by into the now barely there crowd. He's wearing a shirt with a fake tuxedo front and Wayfarer-style Ray Bans.

"Do I even have to guess?" I say, changing the subject away from me.

"Bottom," we say in unison.

Panda joins our little circle and bows. "The most illustrious performer, Bottom, at your service."

"I always knew you were an ass," Richard says, and Panda kisses his cheek. I walk to the bulletin board again. Karen is, in fact, Titania, and Wes is King Theseus, Hippolyta's husband, and as Taft explained during auditions, he's also the fairy king, Oberon.

"I'm starved," Panda says, and reaches into his back pocket for a small bag of potato chips. "Let's celebrate with Burrito Heaven for lunch."

"Ooh, good idea," May says.

"You can't, you're not a senior, remember?" Richard says gently.

"You think that will stop him?" May says just as Karen hurries from around the corner to the bulletin board. She hesitates, pulling back from the list, as curious as I am why Taft split the parts. When she sees me standing there, a smile immediately plasters on her face and she joins May, Panda, and Richard celebrating. They start heading down the hall to sign out at the main office.

"You coming?" Panda calls to me.

"I'm gonna go talk to Taft," I say.

"Go get 'em!" May calls. She cackles in happy celebration. I exhale sharply, surprised by their support. They turn the corner, out of the hallway.

"You will not quit. You will not get a case of the nerves," Taft says, pacing before me. She is holding a piece of paper in her hand with a large hand-drawn blue asterisk.

"No," I say. Taft's eyes dagger at me. "I mean, no, I won't get the nerves. I really want this," I say quickly. I sit in Taft's office chair and she walks back and forth again and again.

"You will not dodge phone calls or ignore your friends. You will not show up late even *once*," she says.

"But!"

She holds up the asterisk and I immediately silence. After years of working every summer with this woman from fourth through tenth grade here at EG and at OSTC, I know she only thinks you're listening if you are looking at her directly in the eyes.

"Maybe it's the fireflies taking over the town and eating all my flowers, but I'm on edge, Berne." She stops pacing and points at me. "I'm giving you a chance, Penny. *One* more chance."

I open my mouth and she shakes the asterisk in my face and continues.

"You will *communicate* if you are still prohibited from driving and if someone else is going to make you late." I don't want to meet her eyes but her expression momentarily softens. "You will use your cell phone to communicate if something is happening at home to make you late." She jumps back into "drill sergeant" mode.

"As you are so wont to do—you will not complain about late rehearsals, itchy costumes, and you will not voice conflict of production approach. Do you agree to these terms?" She places her hands on her hips and I try not to focus on the dot of fresh mustard on her blouse. I can't help it and she looks down. "Oh hell," she says, and snatches a tissue from her desk.

"Do you?" she asks again while dabbing at the spot.

"I do."

With a toss of the soiled napkin, she opens the top drawer in her desk.

She takes out something small that she's able to conceal in her hand.

"Open your palm," she says.

"Is this the part where you strike me with a ruler?"

She erupts into a loud, horsey laugh, but clears her throat immediately and frowns.

"Palm," she demands.

I hold up my hand. In it she drops a white button, and on it is a blue asterisk.

"You made me a button?"

She holds up the button in place of the paper.

"Your final contract requires you wear this asterisk until dress rehearsal," she says.

"So this is my scarlet letter?"

She lowers herself into a chair across from me and all joking leaves her voice.

"No," she says in a low but sincere tone. "It's so you never forget, Penny, how close you came to losing it all. I *know* you don't remember, and I don't fault you for that. But I believe, deep down in your heart, your soul knows what happened that spring and I even know that some of it was out of your control. You don't want it to happen again."

I pin the button on my blouse.

"Well, you don't have to wear it now."

"I want to."

"You are always responsible for your own life, Penny," Taft says. "Even when things happen to you that you can't change, you're in control of how you handle those tough situations."

I stand up. I don't have to wear the pin right now, but it doesn't matter. I'm in the cast. I'm *part* of the cast again. I want to hug Taft, but she's not a hugger. Instead, I grip the door on my way out of her office and make sure to look back.

"You don't want to leave this," she says, and hands me the paper with the hand-drawn asterisk.

I take it from her. "Thank you," I say. "For everything."

"You bet. Now go learn your lines," she says, and points at me with her pencil.

FIFTEEN

THE NEXT DAY, AFTER LUNCH, PANDA, MAY, AND I are in the hallway. We tried to go to the outside tables, but there was a sign on the door that until the "lightning bug" population decreases, the outside cafeteria will be closed. The door to the caff eases closed behind us with a fresh new VOTE FOR KYLIE poster—with yet another photo where I have been digitally removed. I shake my head, take a step, and *freeze*. I wiggle my toes to make sure.

I can feel them!

"What? Did your whole foot go numb?" Panda says. "Do we need to amputate?"

"I can *feel* my toes," I say, and hold out my hand for May to take it—she does. The pins and needles in my right foot *are gone.* I take really small steps from one side of the aisle to the other, making sure to press on the ball of my foot. I walk up and down the hall, smiling.

"Oh my god!" I say with a jump. "Maybe my memory will come back or the figures will fade next."

May hugs me and then Panda does too on top of her so it's one smelly potato chip group hug.

This is the first real indication I've had that I'm healing. When we pull out of the hug, Kylie comes out of a nearby room and puts up another homecoming queen campaign poster. This one has the same picture but with a different slogan that reads: VOTE CASTELLI! HOMECOMING QUEEN 2016!

She rolls her eyes when she makes eye contact with me and turns her back to put up the poster. I gesture to May and Panda so they know I want a minute to talk to Kylie. Maybe it's the new feeling in my toes, but I decide to be brave when I say to her, "You're mad at me for being struck by lightning, for being in the wrong place at the wrong time. That's crazy. I couldn't help it!"

She turns slowly, her arms crossed. She's clenching her jaw. Her features, small and unfairly proportionate, are sharp. "Is that what you think?" she says quietly. "That I'm mad at you because you almost died?"

"Well, when you say it like that . . ."

Kylie huffs and gathers another poster at her feet. She moves down the hall.

"What is it then?" I follow her.

She doesn't answer. I snatch the poster from her to get her attention but she yanks on it too and it rips straight in half. Kylie falls back to the wall.

"I'm sorry!" I say.

"Shit!" she cries. "Do you know how expensive it is to print pictures this big?"

"I'm really sorry. I'll pay for it."

"Of course you will. You'll just fix everything." She snatches her things and hurries down the hall.

"What are you talking about?" I yell, following her. Everyone in the hall is now looking at us, but I'm too angry to care. "Why are you being so *mean*?"

I stop. A new memory comes rushing back. May's voice, *"Why are you being so mean?"*

"What are you even doing here?" I say. She showed up to the party in her best black blouse.

"Come back to the play, Taft will let you," she says. In her eyes is a plea and they keep whipping back and forth between Kylie and me.

"Just go home, May. I'm done," I say.

She pulls me into the kitchen. "Penny, just tell me what's going on. Please."

"I said, go home!"

"Why are you being so mean?" she cries.

Kylie's voice pierces my memory.

"Why am *I* being mean?" she says, repeating my words. "Have you ever thought that it's *you* who's treating *me* like this?"

I shake my head. "What?"

"You're treating me like crap," she says. "I see you trying to get your friends back. You *accidentally* sat at my lunch table and for like, one second, I thought you actually wanted to sit with me. That you would make an effort to be friends again. But, no. Instead I watch you nearly break your back to get your old friends in your life who you were more than happy to ditch a couple of years ago. And I took you in as my best friend. And you couldn't care less that I'm hurt, that I lost *my* best friend, Penny! I—" She stops herself. Kylie wasn't shouting at first, but she is now, and I drop my chin to my chest, my body thundering with the truth of what she is saying.

The noise in the hallway has dropped to a hush. There's light chatter around us; some people even pass by with a giggle.

"You don't care that I don't have anyone to call or ask advice. You don't know."

"You're right," I say, and when I look up, tears are in Kylie's eyes. "I'm sorry. I haven't thought about what you're going through. I just thought, I guess I assumed from how you were acting, that you were angry."

"That I watched you get struck by lighting and nearly die? That I called the hospital and the nurses' station asked if I was some girl named May that you had been asking about. Someone I knew you hadn't talked to in a year? Yeah, I'm mad at you for nearly dying, Penny. That sounds stupid just saying it."

"I don't know what to say," I say, and step to her, but she gestures for me to stay away with the shredded poster in her hand.

"Don't," she says. "I don't want your friendship like this. I don't want it at all."

* * *

"Do you think people might actually come to the show this year?" May says. We sit in the auditorium with our feet on the chair backs in front of us. "Football's been canceled and there's two months until basketball starts. People might actually need something to do on a Friday night."

I keep going over what Kylie said in the hallway.

"Hello? Penny? Friend?"

I groan. "I'm sorry."

"You're distracted. You can't be distracted at our second rehearsal. It does not bode well for Operation Get Your Life Back."

"I don't know how to say I'm sorry to Kylie," I explain. "But I don't know how to be friends with her either. We don't have anything in common." I lean my head back on the chair. "If I could remember, it would make my life so much easier!" I smack my script on the armrest.

"Okay, well, if wishes were horses," May says, and rolls her hand over and over. "Concentrate. You have to run lines with Wes so get your asterisk A-game on."

I nod and draw a deep breath, just as Taft comes out from backstage. She has some tape with her and marks an X on the stage; she walks a bit farther downstage and does the same. She's considering spike marks, for blocking, which seems really early to me. The old me would have yelled that exact thought out to her, but the button on my chest keeps me quiet.

"Okay!" Taft cries. "Let's get Theseus and Hippolyta up here."

Wes, who's in a row a couple down from us, gets up. "May, can you help Thomas with some costumes? He's having trouble locating some doublets."

"Ah yes, tights and breeches. How I love thee, Shakespeare," she says.

Wes and I stand across from each other. "So, as you know when we did the read-through, you two are to be married. This is act five, scene one."

We take a moment to flip to the scene.

"You two read it through together again and feel the emotional beats between the two characters. I'll be back in a minute after you two work on that." Taft walks off, calling for the mechanicals.

"What's with the blue asterisk?" Wes asks, and nods to the button.

I chuckle a little and roll my eyes. "To remind me of my duties as a member of the theater."

"That makes no sense."

"It's a long story. Let's do the scene," I say quickly. "Okay so, act five, scene one is the end of the play. Theseus and Hippolyta disagree about the stories the lovers tell."

Wes looks at his script. "Theseus thinks the lovers are making up the story of the strange events in the forest."

"Right," I say. "And Hippolyta thinks they're telling the truth."

"We're supposed to be at our—" Wes hesitates but it's a fraction of a second. "Our wedding celebrations. After the play within a play."

Wes and I lock eyes and I wish we were back in the woodworking room, our shoulders nearly touching. For a moment, we're both stuck.

"Okay!" Taft says, coming back over. So"—she checks her notes—"this is the moment right after the wedding reception. We'll scatter some people about, have the nobles dancing in the background while you guys have your initial dialogue downstage."

Taft drags a table to the center of the stage.

"Grab some chairs."

We do, and Wes moves his seat to the head of one side of the table, so I follow suit and go to the other end.

"Are you two kidding me? Could you be any farther away from each other? You're married!"

We move quickly to the center so we're sitting side by side.

"Okay, so let's walk through it," she says.

Wes puffs up his chest, which is so *un*Wes, as he takes on the character of King Theseus.

"'Tis strange, my Theseus, that these lovers speak of." I pretend to sip on a goblet of wine.

"More strange than true: I never may believe these antique fables, nor these fairy toys—"

"Wait, wait," Taft says. "You need to show you're married in your body language. I know marriage feels like a million years away for you two, but you get what it means to be in love, right? So *act*."

I panic, but I can't say anything. I promised Taft I would behave.

Blue asterisk. Blue asterisk.

Wes slips an arm over my shoulder and turns his knees toward me. I try to be cool, but my heart pounds and goose bumps trail up my arms and neck. I feel Wes stiffen next to me.

"Better," Taft says. "Try again."

We do, and we only get a few more lines down when Taft calls cut a second time. "Better, but it's forced. You two need to relax. Wes, as you're talking about what the lovers have told you, how might you still show the audience that you love Hippolyta?"

"I might be closer?"

"Yes. And what else?"

Wes pulls me closer, but it still doesn't feel right. I offer the wineglass I am using as a prop. "What if we share the goblet?" I ask, and sit back down.

Taft is really getting going now. "I like that! Try to make sure you're actually feeling it. Don't just say the lines. Think about your motivations, how you *feel*."

"Okay," Wes says, and throws his arm over me again.

At his touch a white burst of light explodes in my mind. It makes me draw my hand over my eyes:

A white wine bottle rolls over the kitchen floor to my feet.

"Bettie. It's my Mom," I cry, and my voice is thick with worry and tears.

I gasp quietly when I blink the memory away. I cough to cover it up and pull the sleeves of my hoodie down over my arms out of nervous habit. I've seen a fragment of that memory before. I recognize Mom's wine bottle.

". . . consider Theseus's backstory. What was it like when

he fell in love with Hippolyta?" Taft is saying. But I didn't hear anything that came before it.

"Can I take five?" Wes blurts out, standing up and quickly moving his body from mine. I have to catch myself on his empty seat.

Taft sighs. "Sure, take a minute. I need more time with the mechanicals anyway." She runs her hand through her frizzy hair when something catches her eye offstage. I turn to look and Chris, the guy who plays Quince, is on Panda's shoulders. "What are you doing? Get down or you'll fall and break your legs and miss the play entirely!"

"I can't concentrate with homecoming tomorrow night. I have to pick up my suit," Chris says, and jumps down.

Taft runs through nine reasons why she doesn't care and I watch Wes hurry up the aisle, and out to the hallway. I don't notice May come up from backstage, but she's next to me and leans to my ear. "Looks like someone *else* is having trouble with Operation Get Your Life Back."

She raises a devilish eyebrow and scoots away to help with costumes. I watch the door ease to a close and fight the urge to follow after Wes. A little part of me smiles inside. He's struggling with the marriage scene. I'm taking that as a good sign. Maybe I'm right and I am finally chipping away at his anger.

Maybe I'm finally getting inside.

SIXTEEN

"YOU GUYS LOOK GREAT," DAD SAYS, AND SNAPS A picture on his cell. May and I stand out in the driveway, waiting for Panda and Richard to show up. She rubs at the goose bumps on her arms. It's early October, and the weather is finally beginning to turn.

I pull my shawl over my shoulders to cover my arms. The only dress I had in the closet is one I apparently bought with Kylie over the summer. It's backless, red, with a long slit. Even though the figures are fading, they are still easily visible on my back. I pull the shawl closer to cover them.

"Do you have to wear the pin on your homecoming dress?"

"I don't *have* to," I say, and reposition it so it's easily seen on my chest. "I want Taft to see it."

The trees and greenery are basically blinking lights in the coming twilight, because of the fireflies coating the trunks and branches. When we check out Dad's digital pic, there are hundreds blinking in the background of the picture.

"You should just drop the shawl," Mom says, coming out of the house. She holds a hand over her wineglass so that no fireflies decide to take a dip in her Pinot Grigio. Every time Mom talks to me, I hear myself calling Bettie and asking for help. I see the white wine bottle rolling across the floor. I don't want to ask Bettie what happened that night; I want to forget it entirely.

I don't *want* that part of my memory to come back.

Then why is this memory the one you keep coming back to? a small voice says, and again, I push it away, deeper into the dark room of my mind.

"Maybe you should just let people see the figures more," May says for the ten millionth time.

"On homecoming night? No thanks."

"She still thinks it's a pity vote," May says to Mom and Dad, and I could smack her.

"Why wouldn't they vote for you?" Mom says, and takes a sip of white wine. "You're the star of the school."

Panda's lime green car zooms down the street.

"Oh good, he drives so safely," Dad says to Mom.

Panda stops at the edge of the driveway; a rap song I don't recognize blasts from the speakers. Once they park, Panda and

Richard get out of the car and of course Richard is the only one dressed in a suit. Panda is in a pair of dress pants and a T-shirt with a tie printed on the front. He also has on his sunglasses again.

"You look dashing!" I cry. "Nice T-shirt," I add, to Panda.

"One more picture!" Dad says. He gestures by showing them the cell.

"Humor him, please," I beg the guys.

"Anything for Queen Hippolyta's family!" Richard says with an exaggerated bow.

"You guys call her the queen now?" Mom says. She looks at me. "I knew you liked to be the center of attention, but don't you think that's taking things a little far?"

My friends look at me awkwardly. A bolt of horror runs through me. I don't have time to stop Richard before he explains. I didn't even realize I hadn't told my friends I was keeping the play a secret from my parents. Everything had happened so fast that it never crossed my mind.

"She's Hippolyta in *A Midsummer Night's Dream*, that's all I meant," Richard says. His tone is casual because he assumes Mom knows about the play. Who wouldn't?

Mom blinks a lot of times and very fast. "I see," she says, and takes a deep sip of her wine. May looks back and forth between Mom and me. Mom places a hand on her hip. "And when were you going to tell us you tried out for the play *and* got a part?"

"Can we talk about this later, Mom?" I whisper.

I don't make eye contact with Richard but I can tell he's horrified.

"We should really get going. I'm always late," Panda says, and takes off his sunglasses. He extends a hand to Mom and Dad, and my friends escape into Panda's car.

Dad kisses my head. "Have a good time," he says.

When it's Mom's turn for a hug, I make sure to say, "With everything going on with the journalists and you and the company—" She cuts me off by hugging me. "It's all right." I pull away quickly and get into the car. "Have a good time!" she calls crisply.

"I'm so sorry," Richard says, spinning around in his seat. The frames of his eyeglasses are black tonight to match his suit.

I squeeze his shoulder. "So not your fault. I just wasn't ready to tell her yet."

When May and I meet eyes, she gives me an encouraging smile.

When we get to school, I have to admit I'm impressed. The gym looks incredible. A huge banner on the wall reads CLASS OF 2017! Blue-and-white streamers and gold twinkle lights hang by the hundreds from the ceiling. A mass of bodies dance to a DJ in the center of the room.

"Kind of a lame theme," Panda says, and makes a beeline for the snacks that line the wall. "School spirit? Like we're all *soooo* disappointed about the football season getting canceled?"

"At least we know they didn't use the football budget on decorations," I say to May as I grab a chocolate-chip cookie. I do a sweep for Wes, of course, but also for Kylie. I really *do* want Kylie to win. There are so many girls in glittering dresses and guys in suits, it's impossible to find her in the crowd.

Richard pulls on May and they immediately head to dance. Panda sits down at a table near the dance floor and munches on his treats. I am about to sit too when Richard and May shimmy over to me.

"Drop your shawl," Richard cries. He shakes his hips and spins on his heels.

"No way."

"It's fourteen hundred degrees in here," May cries.

"Stop peer pressuring her, Bad Seed," Panda cries. Behind me, his crew from the 7-Eleven already surrounds him.

May pulls me to the edge of the dance floor. Richard is an *amazing* dancer and it doesn't take long for a group of people to dance with us. After a few songs, I fan my face with my hand and wipe sweat from my forehead with the edge of my shawl.

With the numbness gone and much of the strength back in my right side, I can dance easier. The exaggerated funky downbeats make me want to swivel my hips.

"Make way!" Panda cries. Leaping up from the table, he does a somersault onto the floor. He jumps up and says, "Ta-da!"

Richard swings his tie above his head. I nearly trip when I catch a glimpse of Wes. He's near the far wall of the room, but he disappears out the side door of the gym, into a hallway.

"I . . . I'll be right back," I say, and edge through the crowd. It takes me a while to get through everyone. I pass Lila, Eve, and Kylie dancing in a tight group near the front stage. I wave timidly at Kylie, and as I expect, she turns her back to me. I step out into the empty hallway. He couldn't have gotten too far.

I find Wes sitting in the weight room by a huge window overlooking the football fields. The twilight sky is a mix of purple and gold with all the fireflies bobbing and weaving through the warm October air. He's wearing a charcoal gray suit that makes the blue of his eyes pop.

"Taking a break?" I say, and walk toward him. The weight room is right next to the gym, so the thumping music is vibrating the mirrors, distorting my reflection.

Wes snaps his head up to look at me.

"Fruit punch and cookies getting you down?" I try again.

He doesn't reply at first, but his lips part just a little. "Wow, Pen. You look great."

"Thanks," I say. "You do too. What are you doing in here?"

"I don't know; homecoming is kind of lame this year."

"Tell me you haven't become a football fan during my lost year."

He laughs. "No."

I lean on the wall near him and cross my arms under the shawl.

"Just, it's senior year. I wanted to go with . . ." And he shrugs, making sure not to meet my eyes. He groans loudly, catching me off guard. I take a step back.

"I can't do this with you, Penny!" he confesses, and stands up. "One minute I'm mad about what happened with us and the next, I'm . . ." He stands across from me and the closeness between us makes me flush. "I want you to remember, and you don't, and I know it's not fair to you to be mad at you for that. You can't control it. It is what it is. That's what happened in rehearsal," he confesses. "If you were wondering."

I'm just glad we're finally coming to it. That's it's finally coming out in the open.

"I was."

"It's like I can't be close to you like that when I'm all messed up about this."

"What *did* happen between us?" I ask, and he looks over my shoulder, out the window to the empty fields. "If anyone can tell me, you can."

He nods.

It's dark in the weight room, but the fireflies outside have made the room glow gold.

Wes has gotten so much *taller* than me. I almost reach up and touch his jaw, but lower my hand. Instead, he lifts his arm and wraps his fingers around mine. His are callused from woodworking. Wes leads me out a door to the fields and my heart thumps when I swallow.

"What are we doing?" I ask.

He walks us across the field until we stand in the direct center.

Wes and I face each other, me in my dress and him in the suit, and the fireflies swell. Thousands flutter around us, in a symphony of light. Up, down, and all directions, they make lattices of light. They make patterns of iridescence. Our eyes are locked—I don't want to talk too loud and break the spell. He brings his hand over my heart and leaves it there. I press my body closer to him and in the space between us, I could kiss him so easily.

"Penny Berne . . ." He says my name and examines my face with a shake of his head.

"I'm still me," I whisper.

He takes the edge of my shawl and tugs it so it falls off my shoulders, exposing the figures I have so desperately tried to hide. We let the shawl pool at our feet. Adrenaline buzzes high in my chest, at the base of my throat. Wes lifts my arm to his eye line. The branches I've been so ashamed of are etched deeply onto my skin, but in this sea of moving light, here, with Wes, it doesn't matter.

No one but Mom and the nurses have touched the figures, but now, here, Wes runs his fingers over the branches on my arms.

"When you quit the play . . ." he says, "you wouldn't talk to me. It was like you quit me too. And I didn't know why, or what I'd done. I thought you just . . . didn't have feelings for me. After I made you the planetarium, things were just different."

When his eyes meet mine, they seem almost gold from the light of the fireflies. He lifts his hand from my chest and I think he's going to hold my cheek. I need to keep touching him. The field might have disappeared for all I notice; his hand rises to cup my cheek. I take a breath, my cheeks flush, and I can't stop the tears coming. I don't know if I want them to.

"You were gone. It was like someone went out and replaced you with robot Penny. I didn't know this icy, vacant girl. *That* Penny wasn't mine. I wanted *my* Penny back." A firefly flies right above our heads, almost illuminating his thoughts. He glances at me and says, as if to himself, "Our Penny."

The tears fall over my cheek and onto his hand. His eyes lift to the dancing lights.

"I think they've stayed for you," he whispers.

He leans forward, closer and closer, his lips coming toward mine.

With a *bang* of the gymnasium side door, we jump apart.

"Holy balls," Panda cries. "You won! Penny, you won! You gotta come!"

"Nice rhyme!" May says, and Panda shoves her back from the doorway.

It doesn't compute at first what they mean. "Homecoming queen!" Richard cries.

Wes and I meet eyes. "Oh my god," I say. "I really won the pity vote."

I jog behind my friends, and only when I get into the raucous cheering and see Tank standing on the stage with a crown on his head do I remember I left my shawl on the field—and it surprises me that I don't want to put it on anymore.

Alex James and Kurt Leonard stand behind Tank. Kylie and Angela, the other girl nominated, stand next to Ms. Reley. Kylie's smiling but it's polite; she blinks hard and often, probably trying to force away tears. Why doesn't this walk to get my crown feel like a victory?

I lift the hem of my skirt as I walk up the steps. I glance back for Wes, but don't see him in the crowd. I know people are clapping, but they are pointing too. My ferns are exposed, copper and gold, under the bright lights.

Ms. Reley reaches behind the DJ table and pulls out a gold tiara. She says something into the microphone about me being the homecoming queen and starring as Hippolyta in the play. I can't hear it all over the applause and cheers.

I bend my knees dutifully as she places the tiara on top of my head. I check the crowd and the people watching us. Eve and Lila stand near a horde of basketball and football players. Eve isn't clapping at all but looking at Kylie and I can't bring myself to attempt eye contact.

Tank runs to me and spins me around on the stage.

"Yeah, Berne!" he cries, and the room explodes in cheers just as he places me down. Lila claps and smiles up at me, and I think that sure, maybe it was a pity vote, but maybe it *wasn't.*

The DJ cries out something unintelligible and a rap song brings everyone to the dance floor again. I walk over to hug Kylie, and just as I lift my hands she passes by me and descends the stairs to her waiting friends. She trails rose perfume and cigarette smoke in her wake—it's an oddly familiar smell, comforting. It reminds me of a rainstorm and I don't know why. But Kylie bows her head while Eve and Lila engulf her in their arms. They hurry her off to the edge of the dance floor toward the bathroom, and when she passes under a light, I can see she has broken down completely, dissolved in tears.

"Penny!" Panda cries. There, in the center of the dance floor, are my friends. May keeps pointing at the space open next to her, gesturing me to get out there. Richard cha-chas like a professional. "My queen, Hippolyta of the Homecoming!" Panda cries.

"Come dance with your subjects!"

I jump from the last stair to the floor, then do a couple of turns and a fake ballet leap to the group of my friends, who wait for me—with open arms.

SEVENTEEN

ALMOST A WEEK LATER, AFTER SCHOOL, I SIT onstage with May, Richard, Panda, and Wes as we paint five of Wes's wooden trees for the fairy realm set.

"I feel horrible," I say. "She wanted to be homecoming queen. I didn't."

"So did I," Richard says, and we all laugh.

"Just let it go," May says. "You won fair and square. Besides, you can't change it now."

Wes is next to me, running a brown paintbrush up and down the trunk to give it texture. I keep trying to find excuses to nudge or touch him.

That morning I had read through a newspaper article that Mom had left out on the kitchen table.

Alice Berne: Back in Action!

Following her daughter's near-death experience, Alice Berne is taking a cue from her daughter and entering back into the spotlight. Penny Berne, a senior at East Greenwich Private and theater enthusiast, just won the role of Hippolyta in this fall's production of *A Midsummer Night's Dream*—

Now, I adjust the newspaper under the tree Wes is painting, making sure the article is carefully positioned under the spot where his brush keeps dripping. A brown blob falls on Mom's face.

"We've already sold two hundred tickets," Richard says, dabbing a sponge in the last bit of green paint.

"It's my sordid reputation," I say.

"Hey," he says. He lightly pats the tree with the sponge to create texture—so it looks like there are a lot of green leaves. "Any publicity is good publicity."

"Taft didn't mention the button yesterday at rehearsal. She's getting used to me again. That's a plus," I say. Wes glances back to see if I am wearing my blue asterisk. I always do—on my chest.

I look out at the empty auditorium and the dozens of fireflies bobbing through the darkened room.

Wes passes by behind me and says, "Don't let her fool you. She's got an eagle eye, dollface."

I am about to tell him to shove it with the dollface when he squeezes my shoulder gently before walking away. In a thud of my heart, the memory, the one I've been seeing in pieces for weeks, rolls through my head again. It's fractured, though, like a blinking light bulb that only illuminates part of a room.

Mom comes in and hip checks the island with her cell phone in hand.

She catches herself on her elbow with a smack.

"Mom, stop it. You can barely walk."

"I'm fine!" She snatches the wine bottle.

"Penny?"

I refocus on my hand holding the paintbrush over the wooden tree.

A firefly in the dark room of my memory weaves out of the blackness toward me, closer to where it knows there is light. Its patterned illumination becomes brighter and brighter with each bob and weave. I wish I could lock the door.

"We need two more cans of evergreen paint," Wes says. "But I gotta go spray the waterproof lacquer on the ones we've already done."

"I'll get it," I say, grateful to get up and move around.

As I get up, I note that the sleeves of my sweater are pushed up near my elbows so the golden figures crawling up my arms are visible. Since homecoming, I've stopped caring. I'm not going to pull the sleeves down. I push them up even higher. I'm not going to be afraid anymore. If my brain wants to haunt me with horrible memories of my mother or the way I treated my friends—fine, I'm different.

I am not afraid of who I am now.

I join Wes backstage. "Two cans are all you need?" Wes throws me a thumbs-up. The hazy lighting illuminates us both from above. I wish that he would follow me to the supply closet. I imagine him close to me. I imagine myself touching his face . . . his lips.

"The other night, at homecoming," I say. I dare to reach out for Wes's hand and take it into mine so they intertwine. He sighs, and lets go gently.

"I just need a little more time," he says. "I have to get used to this new version of you."

"I understand," I say, and take the key. "No problem."

"Penny . . ." he says gently, and I turn back.

"Yeah, Gumby?"

"I want to."

"Me too."

Once I'm in the supply closet, I slide two cans of evergreen paint from the shelves, and when I come out to the hallway, a song is blasting from the school radio station. I step a few feet down the hall and the door is cracked open just a bit. Kylie is on the floor with noise-canceling headphones over her ears. She taps out a rhythm on her hip bones. I knock on the doorway, knowing she isn't going to hear me as she's completely transfixed by the song. I squat down by her shoulder and tap lightly. Kylie kicks back with a scream and throws off the headphones.

"Sorry! Sorry! I did this to Wes too."

Kylie holds her hand to her heart and her long blond hair falls messily in her face.

"I hate you," she says breathlessly.

"You were really into that song."

"Yeah," she says, and gets up. "It's called listening to music." She checks something on a computer monitor. "Oh crap," she says, and grabs the headphones from the floor. She scoots to the microphone and brings her finger to her mouth, signaling me to be quiet. She presses a couple of buttons on the touch screen. A little white light on the screen reads: ON AIR. "That's our local band, Howl, here on 94.1 WEGH. You can see them this Saturday night at the Joint in Westerly. I'll be down there giving away some tickets and swag, so don't miss it. Up next, let's go old-school with The Doors."

The little light goes off and Kylie removes the headphones.

"Wow. You were really good."

"Thanks," she says, and turns to me in the swivel seat. "I've been doing it all year."

I forgot the radio station broadcasts every night until eight.

"You were the one who encouraged me," Kylie says.

"I did?"

"Yeah. You said, 'Kyle, if you don't try, you don't get, so suck it up and do it.'"

"My mom says that," I say.

She punches something into the computer. "I know. But it helped anyway."

I hesitate, then step away from the doorway and into the room.

"Kylie . . . how much *do* you know about my mom?"

"She drinks. Sometimes it's up and sometimes it's down. When she was good, you know, not drinking so much, you would invite me over. I always knew when it was bad, because you kept me away." She pauses. "And she can be hard on you."

"She's having one of those fun *up* moments right now."

"I figured. I saw on the news."

"Did you know," I say, and make sure to check I didn't leave any paint on the door before walking inside fully, "that she went to rehab? I didn't remember, but I found out recently."

"Wow. You never told me." Kylie crosses her arms over her chest.

"Yeah, that was my 'thing,' apparently."

The music from the radio fills the silence.

"I'm really sorry about homecoming," I say. "I wanted you to win. I kept telling May that if I won it was only because it was a pity vote."

"*Totally* a pity vote," she says, and we both find ourselves laughing. "Nah, it's okay," she says. "It doesn't matter anymore. I'm happy for you."

I nod and I'm not sure what to say. I know I can't make this right, and apologizing isn't going to bring my memory back.

"Well, I guess I better get back to the paint."

"Penny," she says when I've turned my back. "I'm glad you stopped in here."

"About the hallway the other day," I say, unable to help myself. "My head is so muddled. I didn't think—"

She squints and frowns, distracting me from my explanation.

She looks like she's trying to work out a problem.

"What?" I ask.

"What's with the blue asterisk?"

"Taft is making me work for my place in the theater."

"Ah." She laughs again. "Hey, want to go to a party at Tank's on Friday? He wanted me to invite you like ten times but you know, I said no."

"Really?"

"No, I'm lying. Yes, really. You can even bring your geeky drama club friends." She's teasing, and the devilish grin on her face makes what she said okay.

"Gee, thanks."

"Seriously. Come."

I nod. It would be good. It would be the right thing to do. Her eyes linger down at my paint-covered hands. But it's only when I see her eyes flicker to the silver ring with the blue stone on her own finger that I realize she was checking to see if I'm still wearing mine. I am, and even though it wasn't intentional, maybe somewhere deep down it was, because I know what Kylie once meant to me.

"I'll see you then," I say. She starts to say something else, but jumps.

"Oh crap! I have to go on air!"

I quickly back out, not wanting to push the moment any more. But when she's giving her next commercial break, Kylie is smiling.

EIGHTEEN

FRIDAY AFTERNOON, AFTER REHEARSAL, DAD HAS a dinner meeting, so it's just Mom and me. I didn't run because of the new icy clip to the early-October air. There hasn't been a frost yet, which has complicated the situation with the fireflies.

I close a window on the browser with my Common App. My entrance essay is almost done; I've got recommendations and a good SAT score. I hope it will get to the important part—*an audition,* a familiar voice whispers. I walk outside to the patio. The icy air hits me immediately. My peach-colored figures have tattooed me for so long, I forget they are there. But with the red-and-brown leaves and the twilight creeping across the sky, they stand out to me this evening.

I turn my arms so I can see the branches curling around them. I thought they would disappear, evaporate, or fade entirely like the doctors said, but like the fireflies, they have lingered long after their expiration date.

It's supposed to snow tonight. Maybe the season for fireflies is ending.

They roam by the thousands, hanging on branches and coating walls of buildings, but I don't want them to go. The forecast is calling for three to six inches of snow. It's hard to imagine that, given how warm it's been all fall, and the bright purple-and-blue flowers of Mom's hydrangeas that are still in bloom.

Downstairs, Mom's assistant from work is droning on and on about the infamous Cenberry wedding that Mom will plan for this upcoming spring. I need to eat something before I get ready to go to Tank's party. As I head downstairs, my phone chimes for the nine millionth time.

MAY: Do I wear pants?

ME: Please. Always wear pants.

MAY: I hate you.

ME: Just wear something you like!

As I make it down to the kitchen I hear a high-pitched, nasally laugh. Oh *god.* I completely forgot how much I hate Laney's voice.

"Penny?" Mom calls. "Is that you?"

She is *way* too happy that I am downstairs. It's never a good sign when she's cheery like that.

"Hi, Penny!" Laney's voice echoes from the living room.

"Hi!" I call back as sweetly as I can. Mom comes into the

kitchen and she looks great. She's blown out her hair and is wearing a bright blue sweater. It's the same style as the one she wore the day I woke up in the hospital, but a different color.

I do a quick sweep for wine bottles, but don't see any.

Laney busts into the kitchen—all fake boobs and frosted hair.

"Your mom told me you got a role in the play. Alice Berne is back and so is her famous daughter? What is the wonder drug this family is taking and where can I get it?" She pretends to look through my pockets.

How do people even talk like this? Laney grabs a chilled bottle of white wine from the fridge, untwists the top, and fills a glass for herself. Why would Laney drink around Mom? She knows Mom went to rehab.

Mom pours herself a glass. "One won't hurt," she says. But we both know she's never been able to stop at just one.

"Well, Penny didn't tell me anything about the role or that she even tried out," Mom says. As she places the wine bottle on the counter, I see that it is the same brand from my memory.

"So, what's the play about?" Laney asks me. I blink away my fragmented memory.

"It's Shakespeare," I finally say, through all my confused thoughts. "Hey, Mom?" I work up the courage to say. "Do you really think you should be drinking?"

"I'm in my own house. I can do whatever I want," she says. Laney looks back and forth between Mom and me. I see her in my mind, lying in the grass, and remember the humiliation that poured over me again and again.

"You know I'm feeling good, I can control myself," Mom justifies to Laney, but I notice that within moments of Mom's excuses Laney is placing her wallet and tablet back into her purse. I'm already embarrassed for Mom.

Mom downs the glass and I realize, when she sways a little on her way to pour another, this *is* the second bottle. There is a smaller half bottle on its side in the sink that I didn't notice at first. She's a little woozy, but not toasted completely.

"Mom. You've had too much," I say.

Laney now has her purse over her shoulder and is getting ready to leave. As usual, I'm going to be left to pick up the pieces.

"You're the child. I'm the mother," Mom yells, pointing her finger at me. Laney moves to the door.

"Let's touch base about the seating chart in the morning. How does that sound?" Laney chirps.

"You have to go?" Mom says in a sweet tone. Laney hugs Mom and then me, but I want to strangle this woman for breaking out the wine when there is so much at stake.

Once Laney leaves, I snatch the bottle from the table in the living room and place it on the kitchen counter. Mom follows behind and grabs it.

"Why are you doing this again?" she says.

"Again?"

She holds on to the bottle tight.

"It's too much!" I cry. "Dad already took you to rehab once."

Mom bangs the bottle on the table and I'm surprised it doesn't crack.

"It's always like *this* with you, Penny."

"Like what?" I say, and reach a trembling hand up to the wall, but for the first time in so long, I feel a sharp squeeze in the center of my palm, threating to draw my fingers together the way it used to. I stretch my fingers wide, so wide it makes the webbing pinch.

She gets up from the table and her hard footsteps land on the floor. Where is Dad? I check the clock—he should be home by eight or so but it's just four thirty. Some wine falls onto the carpet as Mom stomps away from me and up the stairs toward her bedroom. I follow.

"Mom, stop it. We have to talk about this!"

She tries to slam the bedroom door closed on me, but I catch it in time and kick it open so it bangs against the wall behind it. I take the glass out of her hand and she tries to grab it, scratching at the air. "Mom! You can't drink! What about your job? Or rehab? It isn't good for you!"

"It's *your* fault I went to rehab!"

I put the glass down on the dresser, hard. I want to shove all the jewelry off the table. I want to smack the papers so they scatter away.

"Stop saying that!" I cry, and I sound so foolish but I can't find the words. "You drink too much!" Her drunken, slackened mouth disgusts me.

She gets up, moving across the room to get the glass. I should know better. I know better than to follow her and continue this argument. But she needs to hear me. I am going to make her hear me, finally. I won't keep it bottled up inside anymore.

"Listen to me!" I cry. "Do you hear me? You almost lost your business!"

Mom spins and points her finger at me. "Oh no you don't!" she yells. "Don't blame this on me!"

Her face is scrunched up and it's too familiar. I am tight all over, waiting for what could come next, afraid that for the first time in weeks I'm going to have a spasm in my hand.

"You have to stop!" I cry. "For me!"

"I haven't had that much to drink. I don't have to take this from you," she says. Her voice rises to a shriek. "I'm the mother!"

"Just because you gave birth to me doesn't mean I can't tell you how I feel," I scream back.

"I will not let you do this," she says. "You always have to make everything about you. Why do you think I deal with this the way I do? It just never stops!"

I snatch the glass and throw it to the ground so it cracks in half against the hardwood floor. Wine spills across the floorboards.

"Look what you did!" she cries. "You selfish little shit. This is all your fault!"

Memories that were fragmented like kaleidoscopes burst into thousands of colors, smells, washing out the room and making it explode.

I am the shards of glass. I am the fractals of frost peppering the window. I am firewood split through the center. I back away from Mom.

She runs to get more wine downstairs. I sink down to the floor, next to the shards of broken glass.

I can't catch my breath. My ears are ringing. I am in the center of that room in my mind, the shades are up and the light pours in, and the fireflies are nowhere to be seen.

I close my eyes as the memory of that night finally comes, unbidden and unwanted. I know why I quit the play. I know why I pushed my friends away. I know why Kylie saved me.

I remember.

I can't stop shaking. In my bedroom, I sit on the floor, reach under the bed, and slide out Wes's planetarium. A year ago, I slid it under the bed so I wouldn't have to see it every day—so I wouldn't have to be reminded of Wes's unrelenting kindness. So I wouldn't know what I was missing.

I want to be in the pitch dark for this, but the icy air and fireflies outside cast my room in a hazy light.

With a click, I turn it on and the constellations align on my ceiling. I feel my memory settling in the center of my brain and I see the last year so clearly in my mind, like a movie. I watch myself with Kylie and May . . . and Wes. The stars move slowly about the room and my mind churns with all the history I had forgotten.

Mom blames me for everything. Her depression, her drinking—all of it.

There was a time in my life when I guess I let that control me. When I became who Mom wanted me to be. But I'm not that girl anymore.

My cell chimes.

MAY: I'll be there in 10!

I swallow hard, running through the events of the night I quit the play. Mom and I had a fight, I quit, and Dad took her to rehab. Something happened in between. But what? Even though I have remembered so much—there is one small piece missing. One small moment. I knew it.

There is a chime on my cell.

I open my eyes.

MAY: What are you wearing?

I turn off the planetarium so the room goes back to normal. I get off the floor and paint my face with makeup and find my old armor—the designer jeans, the leather bomber. I check my reflection. I look strong. I look like Kylie.

I get it now.

Mom is in her room sleeping it off when I leave.

"What's up?" May asks as I slide into the passenger seat of her car.

"Nothing," I say with a smile. "Excited."

The memory from the night of *that* party with May taunts me:

"Some people weren't invited!" Kylie cackles and the music changes to a dance song. I take Kylie's hand in mine. We dance our way to the middle of the room. I make a spectacle just to show May how much I have changed—that I am not going back to theater.

May and I pull into the party and park next to Panda's car. May is going on and on about the size of the house and I loop my arm through hers because now that I remember, now that I know how much I hurt her, I have no idea how to make it up to her. In the reflection of Tank's door, the blue asterisk pin catches my eye. I need to tell May.

"Don't say anything when we get inside. I need some time. But . . ."

May drops her hand from the doorknob. "What?" she asks. She waits, letting me find the words.

"I got most of my memory back tonight," I confess.

"Oh my god!" She jumps up and down and I want her to think I'm happy too so I hug her first so I don't have to look her in the eye.

"Please don't say anything yet. I'll fill everyone in over the next few days," I say once I pull away.

"Totally," she says, and pretends to zip her lips. She squeezes me as we walk inside.

"If you say you're proud of me for being up-front, I'll stab you with my asterisk pin."

She laughs as the crowd and the music of the party overwhelm the room. I have to be cool and pretend that I don't know that Alex James showed me his junk on the tennis courts, but is now making out with Eve on the couch. Lila dances with Panda and Richard in the center of the room and I don't want to let them know yet that I am sorry for all of the times I kept the conversation superficial and missed out on their friendship. Panda, Richard, even Lila.

This is all your fault.

In some ways, Mom is right. I can leave a damaging wake. Look how much sadness I caused to all of my friends.

"Is Wes here?" May asks. I check my cell to see if he's responded to a text I sent him this afternoon.

ME: You are coming to Tank's party right?

"I don't know. He hasn't written me back yet."

I look at the little time stamp on the text. At 3:15, I didn't remember anything about the last year and then at 4:12, I was sitting on the floor with the planetarium swirling around my room.

"Penny!" Tank cries. He comes out from the kitchen with Kylie riding on his back. She jumps down and hugs me. I inhale her familiar rose perfume and when I pull away I use my hand and pretend it's a microphone. I hold it up to Tank's mouth for an "interview."

"Tell me, Tank. How does it feel to have the key cast members from this year's *Midsummer Night's Dream* here at *your* party."

Kylie smiles bigger than I've seen her smile in weeks.

I hold the microphone under his mouth. "Well, Richard Lewis has made me feel like a tool because I've realized I can't dance."

"No, you can't!" Richard cries from the kitchen where he and Panda are reenacting a scene from the play for some of the people in there. I can tell it's from a scene where Bottom has been changed into a donkey. Tank lifts me up and hugs me and when he puts me down says, "It's good to have you back, Berne."

I glance back at my friends in the kitchen. May has joined Richard and Panda. I check my cell once more for Wes, but there's nothing. Over their heads, I see a glass door looking out to the patio and backyard. I want to go down to the pool. I can't even explain why, but I want to go to the site where I nearly lost my life.

"I'm just gonna go down to the pool a second," I say, and

rezip my leather bomber jacket.

"The scene of the crime," Tank says. "Don't get struck by lightning," he calls when I'm by the door.

May gestures silently, asking me if I want company outside. I shake my head. "I need a second," I say. She nods and I walk down the stairs to the pool. I check for the snow but it hasn't started yet. Instead, the fireflies in the trees light my way.

When I get to the edge of the pool, it's covered up in a blue tarp for the season. I close my eyes and let the tips of my sneakers hang over the edge. The wind throws my hair around. I push my sleeves up because I want the vines exposed.

Someone call an ambulance!

If I let my mind go, I can replay much of the strike.

But someone squeezes my right hand gently.

Kylie's expression is warm. I can tell from the glint in her eye that she absolutely *knows.* She lifts one eyebrow, waiting for me to tell her the truth.

"Since earlier tonight," I say without her needing to ask. "How did you know?"

"Oh come on. Holding a microphone up to Tank. Asking how he feels about the *Midsummer* cast being at his party? Classic Penny Berne. You're back, babe." She laughs. "My number one bitch."

I laugh. "I missed you, Ky."

"I missed you too!"

We watch the hovering fireflies a moment and when I look up to find the stars, it's cloudy up in the sky. "Why so glum?" Kylie asks. "Didn't you get everything you wanted?"

"Not quite. There's still something I feel like I'm missing."

Kylie thinks it over and digs her hands deeper into her parka. I like the fur trim of the hood and think that it would be fun to go shopping together. Maybe she can help me figure out a look that's all mine—not just copying hers. I think I'll always find Kylie the most fashionable girl I know.

She keeps thinking over what I've said.

"What?" I say.

"Well, something must have happened, right? Something must have triggered it. You didn't get your memory back when you were just eating a bowl of cereal or something."

Why must you make my life so difficult! You wonder why I need to cope this way! Who can live like this?

"Well, my mom and I had a really big fight and she said something super fucked-up—shocker—and then I remembered." There's a beat of silence and I add, "I think she needs rehab again."

"What did she say?" Kylie asks. "What was the fucked-up thing?"

"That I'm the reason she drinks. That I make her depressed."

"God, what is wrong with people!" Kylie cries. She's about to go off on one of her rants. "It's like when people said, 'Penny is so different now that she hangs out with you, Kylie. You make her act like a different person.' You can't *make* anyone do anything. You *wanted* to change." She pulls back, reading something from my expression. "You *believe* her? I can see it in your face."

I'm too ashamed to admit it.

"Did you pour the liquid down her throat? Did you force her to drink? Did you *demand* it?"

"No."

"Did you go into her brain and change her serotonin levels?"

"Um, no."

"You can't *make* anyone do anything. It's not your fault."

A surge of love for Kylie shoots through me and I grab her hand again and hold on tight. She's right. I never thought about it like that—never thought about what kind of control I actually had. Mom chose to drink. Mom chose to blame me instead of blame herself. Kylie and I stay at the edge of the pool like that for a minute or two and she turns to me and says, "I'll miss the fireflies, won't you?"

I nod and say, "Yeah, but they're done here. They've moved on to someone else."

She smirks at me and says, "Yes, they have, because you're all lit up inside."

I shove her and laugh. There's a flicker of lightning deep in the clouds. It's not dangerous, but it's high up, near the atmosphere. We both point to the sky at the exact moment. I love that we're both still wearing our matching rings.

There's a crackle of thunder in the air, and a few snowflakes begin to fall softly around us. "Cool! Thunder snow!" Kylie says just as a crash of thunder booms in the sky. I step back, a white bursting light explodes in my eyes, as blue and hot as the day I was struck.

I grip onto Kylie's shoulder as she lifts up her palm to catch the first flakes lightly floating down from the sky. My whole body shakes.

One last memory falls into place. The one I've been hoping for.

Wes and I are at the marina, at our dock.

"I haven't wanted to be friends for a long time," he says. And suddenly, I know what I want. And I know who I am.

"Kylie. I gotta go. Tell May."

"Go? Go where?"

I smile big and turn to run around the side of Tank's massive house.

"Go get him!" Kylie calls.

But I barely hear her—I'm already taking off.

NINETEEN

I JUMP IN MY CAR. I'M RECKLESS AS I ZIP AROUND corners and honk at pedestrians to get out of the way. People walk all over Main Street, excited about the first snow, but I am on a mission.

I have to find Wes.

I send him a bunch of texts, but he never answers. I'm at a stoplight at the bottom of the hill that leads up to school. If his car is in the lot, that means he's up in the auditorium, working on sets.

The air is still thick with fireflies that hover around the streetlamps. More lie like moths against the houses, emitting tiny bursts of light. Halloween decorations and oversize pumpkins line the streets and storefronts. The air is getting colder. Snowflakes continue to fall.

I zoom up to the parking lot but I don't see the Mustang. I pull past his house, my house, Panda's house, and even the woodshop place where he gets his supplies.

As I sit at a traffic light three blocks from Main Street, it occurs to me where I should have looked from the start.

I may have stopped going to the dock, *our* dock—but maybe Wes hasn't.

I slam on the brakes at the end of the block nearest the marina. I think I'm parked illegally but I don't care.

"Wes!" I yell his name even though I'm not quite at the marina yet.

I run past the harbor, past people putting up stupid witchy decorations and buying Halloween candy. I wipe snow out of my eyes as I run faster and faster, like I did before the strike. I want to hold him in my arms, tell him thank you, thank you for coming back to me. For believing in me. For wanting to read the journal my dad gave me and for helping me piece together my life.

For forgiving me even when he didn't have to.

I stop at the end of the dock. The snow makes patterns of swirls in the air.

And there. Sitting at the edge of the dock with a closed sketchbook in his hand is Wes. I step down the ramp slowly, digging my hands deeper in my pockets. I want him to know that yes, I am me, the girl he knew, but I am different now too. I am the girl who finally gets that no one else gets to define who I am or what kind of person I am on the inside.

At the sounds of my feet on the metal ramp, Wes turns.

Confusion crosses his face and he shakes his head.

"Shouldn't you be at the party with everyone?" he asks.

I sit on my knees and nod.

"What's going on, Penny?" he asks.

I cup his strong face in my hands. We are inches from kissing when I whisper, "I had to see you. It's *always* been you. I can say it now."

"What are you saying?" he says, trying to catch up, but he presses his hand on my thigh.

"It's okay to kiss me now," I say. "See? I'm not crying."

His eyes brighten in realization but I lean in to kiss him before he can say anything else.

It's everything I thought it could be. His chest rises at the connection of our lips. I press my hands into Wes's strong back and I know with certainty that I have never loved anyone so much.

Wes accepts me for who I am. He loved me with my memory, and without it, and everywhere in between. I will love him forever for that lesson.

When we pull apart, Wes leaves his hand on my cheek.

"Took you long enough," he says softly.

I move in to kiss him once more, but Wes stops me, pulling at the collar of my leather bomber. *"Look,"* he says.

I unzip the jacket fully to my button-down shirt. My fingers fumble to get it off as fast as I can. I don't care that it's freezing. I twist and turn in my cami to look at my skin. The Lichtenberg figures. The branches and vines that have crawled up my arms and to my chest and my collarbone for months.

They are gone.

The doctor said they would fade eventually.

"I want to tell you. The whole thing," I say to Wes.

I launch into the whole story. From tonight, and before tonight, and even before the strike.

He knows me. He knows me better than anyone.

When I finish, I stand up and Wes follows. "You want to go back to the party? I'll go with you," he offers.

"I think I need to go home," I say. I need to hug Mom. For me and for the past I'm just beginning to figure out.

We walk back to Main Street together and stop at my car.

"I guess there's a lot more we have to talk about," I say, turning to face him.

He leans into me, sliding his hand onto my cheek again. "We have time," he whispers, bringing his mouth to mine again.

When I get home, the kitchen smells like a cinnamon candle, which means Bettie came earlier to check in. Dad is asleep or in the basement working. I blow the candle out and find Mom in the living room—her feet resting on an ottoman. She sips tea. Alice Berne business cards surround her on the couch. She's working, and from what I can tell she looks relatively sober.

I lean in the doorway.

"Is this for the Cenberry wedding?" I ask.

She sighs and eyes me over the top of her magnifiers. "Of course," she says, and the agitation of our fight is still in her voice.

I sit down on the edge of the ottoman. I watch her and the deliberate curve of her French-manicured nails. She smells like Chanel but it's faded after a whole day.

I get up and sit down next to her on the couch, drawing my arms around her and pulling her close to me.

"Don't sit on the cards," she says.

"Mom . . ." I say, and hug her even harder.

I hold on and squeeze and don't let go. She keeps the pen in between her fingers but eventually slips her arms around me too.

I hug her for the little girl in my bedroom.

I hug her for the times I wished she had looped her arms around me and did not.

I hug her for the times she will fail me in the future.

"What's going on?" she asks. She runs a hand up my arm and gasps. "They're gone. The figures."

I let her think this is about my figures. I let her think whatever she wants.

I squeeze her just a little bit tighter.

I don't let her go.

Nearly three weeks later—on opening night of *A Midsummer Night's Dream*—the lightning bug population disappears for good.

The TV reports all say the same thing: *"In a strange migration, the lightning bug infestation that nearly incapacitated the small state of Rhode Island has moved south. Dying out along the way, many of them didn't make it, but some states are reporting an influx of them as far south as South Carolina."*

"Twenty minutes, twenty minutes!" Taft cries, and her hair is coming out of its bun. She points to a couple of the stagehands as they carry Wes's gorgeous trees to ready them for the scene change between the first and second act. "There should be two more," she yells.

I stand by the door of the fitting room in full costume as Queen Hippolyta. My gown is lace like a wedding dress, with a long train. Panda walks by behind me, bringing with him the familiar scent of cheddar cheese chips. I finish the tight bun on my head with one last spritz of hairspray.

Mom and Dad are in the audience, sitting next to Bettie and her family. While I know Mom will make any acting program I get into a part of her "success" and Dad will struggle to get Mom the help she needs, I am okay with it. I have to be because they love me, but are *never* going to change. And I don't have to be the one to fix everything. I can have help.

I need to change—I already have.

Panda throws an arm over my shoulder. He offers me a chip. "Kylie is in the audience. She's sitting with Tank in the third row."

"She's my biggest fan."

"She's totally *my* biggest fan. She wants me to do an interview about the OSTC internship on her radio show," he says. "I agreed, for a small fee."

"What's that?"

"She gets me Blue Indigo tickets for Carl's birthday. He has the night off from the 7-Eleven and they're his favorite band."

I don't ask Panda if his parents are in the audience because we both know the answer to that question. I do know that Carl is in the row behind my parents.

"It's a full house," May breathes, and loops her arms around my waist. She looks amazing as Hermia. We have a similar updo and I offer her the hairspray. She takes it and Panda checks his Bottom costume in the mirror. He has to wear a dirty shirt and tights so I guess it doesn't matter that he cleans his fingertips of the cheddar cheese on his black tunic.

Richard walks by and holds up a hand like a visor. "I am going to pretend I didn't see that!" he cries.

"Penny?" Wes's voice. When I turn to him, he's got a little sweat on his forehead. His hair has grown out so it's nearly in his eyes.

"Remind me not to build sets again," he says. May and Richard pass us.

"Until this summer?" I say, knowing full well he'll be working at OSTC again. Hopefully, we both will. Ms. Taft runs by with an armful of playbills.

"They need more!" she says to us. "Can you believe it? Sold out!" Wes and I laugh because her headset is askew and her bra strap is nearly hanging off her shoulder as she uses her butt to push open the door to the hallway.

Once Richard and May are past us and Wes's back is facing May, she turns around and wags her eyebrows up and down. Richard makes a kissy face and I swear we're all nine years old trapped in high school seniors' bodies.

Wes has a little brown shopping bag in his right hand.

"Come outside with me, dollface?" he asks.

I make a sweeping motion down the front of my dress. "I'm in costume, Gumby."

He does the same sweeping motion. "So am I," he says, except all he has on is the blue gauzy shirt he has to wear as Oberon. He's still in jeans.

"This will only take a second," he says.

Wes leads me out to the hallway. In the opposite direction of the tickets and refreshments table is a second door that leads out to the far side of the football fields. It's cold outside. Wind blows through the lace sleeves of my costume, and the grass crunches under our feet from the recent frost. We stop in the center, near where we stood a few weeks ago, and face one another again. This time, the sky is filled with stars and I look for any evidence of the fireflies, but don't see a single one.

Wes bends down to the brown bag and pulls out a book and hands it over to me. I take it between my hands and feel with my fingertips the deep grooves of an engraving on the cover.

"I'm still learning how to use the engraving tool," he says, and points at the quote he has carved into the cover of a brand-new leather journal. The quote reads:

"Hear my soul speak: The very instant that I saw you, did my heart fly to your service."—William Shakespeare

"I love it," I say, and hug the journal to my stomach. "You made this?"

He laughs a little. "Yeah, Penny. I made it."

I step to him, closing the space between us. He reaches for me, sliding his hands around the small of my back and drawing me near.

Our breath escapes in little white puffs. Our noses are almost touching.

He examines me and an expression, almost like pain, crosses over his face.

"I missed you," I say.

"You have no idea," he whispers. I place my hand at the back of his head and draw him deeper. His arms tighten around me.

The lightning bugs are gone but this kiss is *fire.*

The door slams open behind us and Richard cries, "Get a room!" We pull apart but remain entangled in one another's arms. Panda and May follow Richard out onto the chilly football field. "Taft is asking for you," Richard says to Wes.

"Ten minutes until curtain," May says.

"Besides hooking up, what are you guys doing out here?" Panda asks, and as he's about to peer into the bag, Wes and I step apart. Wes reaches inside and lifts something out.

Cupped between his hands is a Mason jar. Inside, two fireflies pulse and buzz inside the glass.

"No *way,*" I say.

"How did you find them?" Panda asks.

"They were zooming around backstage," Wes replies.

"The last two fireflies," Richard says, and the pin-size lights illuminate the pupils of his eyes behind his thick glasses.

Wes hands over the jar. "You do the honors," he says in that familiar deep voice.

"Go for it, Penny," Panda says, and nuzzles up to me on my right side.

Wes, May, and Richard hug around me on my left. I unscrew

the top and when I open up the Mason jar, the tiny lights bounce out and into the air. I expect them to go separate ways, to go into the world on their own.

But they don't.

They fly side by side, in loopy curls, higher and higher into the sky.

Richard checks his watch. "Shoot, we gotta go," he says. "Or Taft might die."

Wes reaches out for my hand, linking his fingers with mine. I carry the journal under my arm as we walk back to school. Richard gets to the door first and when it opens, we hear the school band *just* beginning the opening number.

I glance back, searching for the lightning bugs one last time. They have moved together toward the tops of the trees. I do a double take.

"Look," I whisper, and point upward. "Look at that!"

The two hazy lights hop through the air to join *three* other fireflies hovering near the start of the woods. They seem to be waiting for the other two.

"*So* cool," May says, and I can hear the smile in her voice.

"Kinda poetic," Richard says lightly, and slides a hand around Panda's waist.

"Softies," Panda grumbles, and we all laugh.

Wes lightly squeezes my hand and I am last in line to follow my friends back inside for our performance.

Panda recites the first line of the last speech of the play as he disappears inside.

"If we shadows have offended, think but this and all is mended."

To be brought back together, to be reconciled, I had to lose myself in the shadows and find my way back out to the light.

I need one last look at the fireflies before heading backstage.

I glance over my shoulder and all five points of light fly higher and higher until I can barely see them anymore. But I follow their steady glow like beacons until they are so far up in the sky that they are soon indistinguishable from the brilliance of the stars.

ACKNOWLEDGMENTS

I'M GRATEFUL TO MY EDITOR JOCELYN DAVIES. This book only exists because of your keen eye and collaboration. You always know how to inspire me to write the best story possible. Thank you.

Thank you, of course, to my agent, Margaret Riley King, who tells it to me straight. You have an awesome editorial eye, and I so value your feedback and loyalty. A big thank you to Erika Niven, who always points me in the right direction!

Thank you to Anna Deroy, who loved my first book and made all of this possible. I promise, one day, I will try to find a way to pay forward this life-changing opportunity.

Thank you to the incomparable and generous CCW's: Mariellen Langworthy, Claire Nicogossian, Linda Melino, Rebecca DeMetrick, Maggie Hayes, Ashley Bray, and Tracy Hart.

There are always so many people who make a book possible. Some of them are Hannah Moderow, Kristin Sandoval, An Na,

Katie Caramiciu, Jennie Maizel-McKiernan and my friends at the amazing Writing Barn in Austin, Texas.

Last, but certainly not least: A.M. Jenkins. You told me to "go there." You said, "write it, don't be afraid. If you don't feel it, neither will your characters." Thank you, Amanda.

For everything.

If you are worried that a loved one is suffering from a substance abuse problem or mental health issue, you are not alone, and it's not your fault.

Consider contacting a school counselor or other trusted adult, or check out one of these reputable sources:

NAMI—National Alliance on Mental Illness:

www.nami.org

Helpline: (800) 950-NAMI

Info@nami.org

M–F 10 a.m.–6 p.m. EST

Al-Anon/Alateen—a program for teens and children of those who are problem drinkers

www.al-anon.alateen.org/

Call: (888) 4AL-ANON